HIGH ON BLOOD AT THE END OF THE WORLD

by Joel Kaplan

Published in Sarasota

ISBN: 978-0-615-69652-2

Copyright ©2012 by Joel Kaplan

First edition published by Kaplan Publishing

Table of Contents

Chapter 1
The Death of Disco, or Werewolves Anonymous

A red cow stood in Frank's driveway. Shit like this happened every day. He sighed. He did not like it. He had noticed the cow out the window earlier. It mooed when he'd opened the curtains for a look at it. Frank thought, *someone must be on their way to get it, cows are expensive.* He forced a smile, determined not to let the cow get to him. It was Saturday, after all.

He'd been looking forward to today ever since he bought those mushrooms. Saturday was mushroom day.

He put a Sonics record on the turntable and smiled as the hiss of the needle gave birth to rock 'n' roll. Much easier not to think about that old red cow now. "Boom" was a record that always lifted his spirits. The upbeat sounds of 1966 demanded to be blasted as the proto punks hammered out pure rock 'n' roll gnosis.

He did not know it yet, but Frank was dialed into something cosmic. It might be a certain record, book, or movie, or anything else, but sometimes it would hit him just right and he'd get a peek behind the curtain. Catch a glimpse of the future and know that he was connected to a malignant otherness he'd never be able to understand, but he did recognize it in certain others. That was the only rationale he had for explaining the feeling that overtook him when a certain scene or a song would hit him in just the right spot. These things held a lot of value for Frank.

He planned the psychedelic escapade for Saturday so Disco could join him. He stood in front of the mirror and greased his curly blonde hair back in a makeshift pompadour, ready to strut on over to Disco's apartment with the half ounce of fungi in his backpack. He looked around the kitchen for something that might distract or win over the cow in case it was feeling aggressive, but all he found was a purple onion. He moseyed out the door with it and the giant red cow mooed again.

"Listen up, cow, it's onion time. Yum, yum," he said, stretching his pale hand out. The cow chomped down the large onion in two bites and stared at him.

"Not bad, huh. Maybe you're not such a bad thing after all," Frank said, pausing to pat her nose before rolling on down the line.

Frank walked down Water Street. He was used to walking around town, and it felt good to stretch his muscular legs. The sun felt good on his black clothing in the chilly November weather of central Maine.

Frank was looking for a good time and nothing more, though soon there would be a lot of death and the whole world would change. But before the changing of the world something happened in Augusta, Maine. Something that changed everything forever, and Frank was going to play a part in that.

Frank was your typical white male in his early twenties, just better looking. He loved sex, drugs, rock 'n' roll, and the Devil. He didn't let the constant stream of bad news on the TV and in the papers get him down; he had his own ways of coping with the current events. He had his own natural disasters to worry about.

Frank walked up the sidewalk to Disco's apartment building at 5:15 PM. It was fated to be Frank and Disco's last hurrah. He rang the buzzer outside the security door three times, which was the custom for friends to announce themselves. Disco buzzed him in and Frank walked up the stairs to the second floor apartment. He scratched on the door and it opened.

"Hey," Disco said in a gruff voice, and motioned him to step in. He was wearing only knee-length camouflage shorts and his black hair was up in perfect tri-hawk. He was only 5'4" and looked like a mini Sid Vicious with muscles.

"Good to see you, Disco," Frank said.

He walked in and flipped his backpack around and pulled out the large freezer bag with the mushrooms.

"Check it, Disco, we're gonna trip our faces off tonight, man," Frank said while holding the bag out. "Tonight there is no coming baaaaaack."

Frank's voice lilted higher as he drew out the syllables. Disco cheered and jumped up and down. "Oh yeah, we gonna get fucked up, Frankie. Would you like to see my new dance?"

"Lay it on me."

Disco gave a big cartoon smile and waved his arms and legs in a dreamy Charleston sort of way.

"You like that. That's good, huh?" Disco said, continuing to dance around the room. He stopped periodically to grab his crouch and point at the ceiling.

"Uh, yeah, man, that's cool. So what's the plan tonight?"

Disco stopped dancing and took a bong hit, considering this.

"You want a clove, Frank? There's not enough space here for mushrooms. We gotta get out of this city. We're gonna go rock it at my camp," Disco said, holding the glass water pipe out to Frank.

"Sounds like a plan. We must fortify ourselves for this journey. I'll take a clove for the ride," Frank said after his hit. He poured out half the bag onto the table and they gulped the mushrooms down.

"You know I once had a dream that you were smoking a five foot clove. Imagine that. Five fucking feet and you were just puffing away at it," Disco said, and tossed him the black cigarette, which he stuck it behind his ear.

"Nasty bastards!" Disco complained, sticking a big spoon full of peanut butter in his mouth to cover the taste of the mushrooms.

"Pussy, you must taste the tribal ecstasy of being alive," Frank said, but he couldn't keep a straight face and he gagged and started laughing. "You're right, they are nasty bastards. I don't know why, other mushrooms are so delicious."

Disco pulled on a yellow Cramps t-shirt. He grabbed a duffel bag and they went out to his 1965 cherry red Chevy Nova.

"That's a real boss hoss, Disco, where the hell did you get that?" Frank said.

"Who cares? You only live once right? This is my dream car, and now it's mine."

"I guess so, man. Let's see what this bad boy can do."

They peeled out and raced down the back roads to Disco's camp with the windows down and the stereo cranking out the sleazy raw noise of Nipple Violator, Maine's best offering of punk filth.

Disco's camp was out a couple of towns over, in Hallowell, and belonged to his family. He knew it would be free and a better place for a mushroom trip. They were starting to feel the effects and it was making them giggle at everything.

"I want your nipples to sew on my body!" the radio screamed, and that set them off. They couldn't stop laughing. Tears were rolling down Frank's cheeks and he wiped them with his hand as they pulled up to the camp. The mushrooms were KICKING IN.

"This is going to be great. No one will bother us out here," Disco said in a voice that sounded oddly plaid, and unlocked the cabin door with a key he retrieved from under a rock with a turtle painted on it. The turtle was running his little ass off. After he unlocked the door he returned the key to its hiding place with what seemed like a fifty foot arm. "We'll chill out for a while. Maybe I'll get a couple chicks out later. I got one more surprise though."

Disco ran back to the car and returned with an expensive bottle of absinthe.

"Cheers, bitch!" Disco yelled, and took a huge haul off the bottle. They passed the bottle back and forth a few times and decided to watch a movie while they ate the rest of the mushrooms.

Disco threw "Fire Walk with Me" in the DVD player and the credits were rolling when a pounding on the door broke their spell.

They looked at each other and both proclaimed, "Oh, fuck!" They were tripping really hard and absinthe drunk and didn't feel up to dealing with this angry lunatic that was also now screaming obscenities.

"It's fucking Bob, man. He's at the fucking door Disco. He killed Laura Palmer and now he's here to fuuuuuuck your shiiiiiit uuuuuuuuup," Frank said, thinking of the movie, and cringed as if he were a mime.

"I don't think I can handle this, Frankie," Disco said. He walked over to the wall and reached for a baseball bat as the door burst in.

A big man in a brown suit cascaded through the broken door with a giant chrome revolver in his hand. He had big, thick black sideburns and was wearing aviator sunglasses, even though it was after sunset. His voice was low, guttural, and menacing. "My money right now or you die, you worthless little pukecicle!" the man said.

Disco's mouth was wide open in disbelief. The man walked forward, putting the end of the gun in Disco's mouth.

"Last chance, faggot," he barked.

The newcomer had been so focused on Disco when he came through the door he had not noticed Frank on the other side of the room.

Frank was tripping so hard he was no longer scared in any way and realized he was just a flesh robot programmed by instinct for survival. He crept forward and nimbly hoisted the now empty absinthe bottle off the table. He swung it with everything he had into the side of the man's head.

The intruder dropped to the ground and his gun flew across the wooden floor and spun under a cot. He was down but not out.

"You're a dead man mother f—," was all the man got out before they started kicking him with their military style boots. Frank stepped up and punted him a good one on the chin. He was out now.

Disco screamed, "We gotta get him outta here!"

Frank screamed, "Okay!"

They each grabbed an arm and dragged the intruder outside of the cabin. They didn't know what to do, so they just dragged him into the woods.

The man started to wake up and they beat him down again. They left him bleeding on the ground in the woods and ran.

They were afraid to go back to the cabin, so they kept running through the woods until they were gasping for breath and all scratched up from the bushes.

"You want to explain that to me, Disco! What the fuck did I just get myself involved in?" Frank said. He shoved Disco to the ground and shook his head.

"I'm sorry, man. I didn't think Jack Valenti would be back in town so soon, and I didn't think he knew about the camp. Don't worry, we're in this thing together, and I'm gonna make it right. I'll give him his money back, plus generous interest, and he'll forget all about it. Bake you a forgiveness cake even probably. No big deal, I swear. Easy peasy," Disco said. He stopped talking all of a sudden. They heard a loud growling sound.

"What the fuck now?" Disco said.

Frank just shrugged and made a face. A loud howl ripped through the night.

"I swear this is the last time I do mushrooms. I'm going to stick with making lists and writing names all over the place," Disco hissed, citing an inside joke of no consequence.

"You're lucky I am this fucked up or I'd be way more pissed at you. I do in fact have to fucking piss," Frank said.

"Shut the fuck up. I hear the train a coming," Disco whispered.

Frank turned to the side and unzipped his fly in time to see a monstrous wolf creature coming right at him, giant and walking like a man.

Warm urine rushed down Frank's leg, leaving a dark patch from his crotch to his ankle. He hadn't had time to get his equipment out.

"Hey . . . uh . . . how's it going?" Frank stammered stupidly.

Disco grabbed a large stick off the ground and hit the wolfman with it. It broke over the monster's back.

The feral abomination picked up Disco and bit his head off. The head tumbled to the ground as the wolfman held up the rest of Disco like he was a big slam of Mountain Dew instead of a headless corpse and gulped the blood. He tossed the body aside and looked at Frank. Frank opened his mouth, about to say something else stupid and the wolf ran off.

Frank stayed there with Disco's body for about ten confusing thoughtful minutes then started running again. He had to find a safe place to hide out and get his head straight.

Chapter 2
We Now Return to the Nightmare on Elm St.

Come on, come on, one foot in front of the other, that's it, Frank told himself, repeating the mantra in his head. Focusing on the repetitive motion. He was exposed walking the streets of Augusta. He had made it a couple miles out of the woods and now was tuned into a primordial fear of the sky, a fear of some great and terrible bird looming in that night sky, capable of swooping down and stealing him away like what had happened to Disco.

Each car that flew by him made him feel more miserable than the one before. Paranoid and disheveled, he was grateful to take that familiar last left onto Elm Street. He was bathed in the darkness, walking past the burned out streetlights. The barn was only a few houses down on the left.

Frank filled his lungs with the smooth night air, knowing he had made it once again. He basked in that oh so familiar victory for a moment. Sometimes it's the simple things in life that you enjoy, like getting where you're going without being arrested. He heard voices and saw shapes on the lawn in front of Lia's apartment building.

He saw five overlapping figures in the grass. He walked up the driveway, passing the groping people.

He made it to the door when a pretty blonde he had never seen before sauntered up.

She demanded a kiss. He could not afford for his entrance to be jeopardized so he complied.

She stumbled into him and they kissed in a sloppy, awkward embrace. It was like they were bottles of blood being poured back and forth into each other, Frank noted, feeling clinically detached. She smiled up at him and shuffled off back to the others on the lawn.

Having paid the gatekeeper, he entered the door and walked up the stairs to the barn. It was his regular hangout, and he felt good to be there. He felt like Godzilla.

Frank was safe in the barn, and the relief was still washing over him like a hot shower. It was better than the kiss, and more sanitary.

The barn glowed from a subdued red light and several strings of blue X-mas lights on the walls and hanging from the rafters. The Electric Hellfire Club pulsated satanic panic industrial out of a boom box on top of an old yard sale record player.

He ascended the black corridor of stairs and turned to open the red cooler on the floor and extricate a bottle of Mad Dog wine from the sea of ice chips. It was death flavored grape, and his mouth tasted like a wino's in no time. He looked around the room and felt heartburn coming on like the drunk mother of a friend.

A broken refrigerator painted a flurry of different colors stood in one corner, next to a painting of a tree hanging on the wall. The branches always seemed to sway. The room lurched back and forth. He didn't see any other people yet.

He sat down on a bench and chugged the wine. He lit a cigarette. He could use a few minutes to compose himself, having just witnessed his friend's death by bizarre animal attack. He detected some movement out of the corner of his eye and noticed there was someone on the mattress in the corner, but the light was too dim for him to make anything out for sure.

Lia slithered into the barn from her adjoining apartment via a rickety saloon style door. She looked very alluring in a blue mini skirt, her stripy tights being swallowed by big black boots. The patterns on her tights swirled in his dilated eyes. She looked like the picture perfect Goth beauty, but he knew she was a whole lot more. Frank smiled and put his hand on her knee.

He fired up a hand rolled smoke for her as she held her hands up to shield her light sensitive eyes that were clamped shut behind her glittering red plastic horn rimmed rhinestone sunglasses. Her hair was an unnatural red that flashed as he flicked the Bic.

"Hey, I'm glad you showed up. I might need you to go on a booze run for me later," Lia said.

"That's cool."

"All the tigers are gone. I heard it today on the radio. That's the latest."

"Whoa, that's sad. They were majestic creatures."

"Pretty kitties," Lia said, growling, and took a playful swipe at his arm.

"So what about all the tigers in zoos and shit. There's got to be a couple left right?"

"All the ones in captivity suddenly died. They're blaming some kind of feline virus."

"It must be that same virus that brought on all these earthquakes and fucking tidal waves, right? It's all so retarded. How can they expect us to believe this shit? That's terrible, though. That really bums me out."

"It was a long time coming. Oh, you'll like this, though. They said on the news that all the disasters were because we were entering a new Tectonic age and it was all normal for this to happen every hundred thousand years or so."

"That's total bullshit and you know it. Too funny. It's the end of the world. Everyone knows that. You know what I think? All those rich asshole politicians and other assorted richies think the joke's on us and they will go off into space and leave us all here to die, but I have some bad news for those pricks. There's even worse shit in space, I bet. It's a fucking Lovecraft universe, you know. I'd rather party here on the sinking ship while the band plays on than get eaten by some cockroach from Venus," Frank said. "Know what I mean, Lia?"

"I think I do, mister," Lia said, and held up her wine. They clinked bottles. "Welcome to the party at the end of the world."

Lia paused for a moment, as if anticipating bad news, but could not avoid the subject any longer. "So where's Disco? I thought you both were gonna come by tonight?"

"Disco's dead."

"Another one bites the dust," she said, and let out a tired sigh. "So how did it happen?"

Frank filled her in on the wild tale, omitting only him peeing his pants, figuring she couldn't tell in the dark barn.

"It just fucking figures. It just fucking figures," Lia slurred, and stumbled over to the corner to snatch up a newspaper. She handed it to Frank. The front-page headline read "Werewolves Definitely Do Not Exist Says Mayor." Frank laughed out loud.

"I guess I'm not the only one with an experience like that then, thank the Lord Lucifer. Oh these end times are zany. What will they throw at us next?"

"Sometimes you have to kiss the snake and sometimes you have to ride the goat," Lia said. "I wanna meet a werewolf, though. That's kinda cool, I'm jealous. It's too bad and all about Disco, but he lived longer than I ever thought he would."

"I was convinced he was going to blow himself up with that grenade you got him for his birthday."

"Hey, I know how to get it on, and I can really throw a party," Lia said.

"Oh I don't think there was ever any doubt of that," Frank said, and laughed. Then the mushrooms made him introspective so he ran on.

"Some important shit is going to go down soon. I feel it in my bones. Things are not right with the world today."

"You might be right. Remember when we used to always tell Disco that he had been to Vegas?"

"Yeah after a while it almost seemed real."

"It just goes to show you everything is just perception, just how an event is perceived."

"True enough. I guess it's also true what they say, Disco's dead."

"Well at least there wasn't another goddamn earthquake in Augusta today. We could all be dead."

"Honey we are on a one way trip to Shitsville."

That was enough talking and they continued to drink in silence, wondering if at any moment the earth would split open and swallow them whole or some kind of monster wolf might come crashing inside and eat them.

That night, they were safe.

Chapter 3
Hitching a Ride

Frank woke up disoriented and very confused. His head was a throbbing, pulsating crown of pain riding his body. There was dirt and blood caked on his hands and he had no idea where he was. It was a dark place with some beams of light coming in between wooden slats, but that was all he could tell.

He had no memory of anything past the barn with Lia.

It was a goddamn cold November, and he shivered in his black jeans and zippered hooded sweatshirt. Oh great, another day filled with mystery.

Frank knew he had to leave and he shuffled over to the door. He walked outside and guessed it was around five PM. He didn't like that; he had been gone too long. He bent down to rinse his hands in a puddle. He had been inside of a small shack that stood alone by the edge of a cemetery. It was strange he did not recognize the cemetery, which meant he must be outside of Augusta.

The wheres and whys of the situation weren't as important as getting away, and he walked toward the one road he could see. He did not know what he might have been up to; all he knew was it was his responsibility to himself to get away clean. He reached into the back pocket of his jeans and pulled out a black plastic comb.

He combed his hair as best he could without a mirror as he limped forward, stretching his cramped muscles. Soon he reached the side of the road with his thumb out.

In eleven seconds flat a black sedan flew by him. It screamed to a halt on the side of the road. Frank smiled and walked over through the dust cloud. First car to drive by. How many times does that happen?

Loud black metal was blasting from the black car's odd blue doors and that made him smile. He saw two teen girls in the car. Frank opened up the back passenger door and got in. The car reeked of skunk bud.

"My saviors. Thanks for the ride ladies. I dig the tunes also, old Venom. I am impressed," Frank said.

"We thought you looked like a rock 'n' roller," the girl driving said, and the girls laughed.

"I just woke up in a graveyard and I don't have any idea how the fuck I got there."

"For real, man?" the girl asked.

Frank smiled. The day was improving. The girl driving had hair dyed bright red held back into pigtails with plastic clips. The girl next to her had choppy blue-black hair. They were both very attractive girls who were dressed like they knew it.

"Are you heading into town?" the redheaded driver asked.

"Which town?" he asked, hypnotized by cleavage.

The black haired girl giggled.

"Augusta, of course," the first continued. She was the talker.

"Must be my lucky day," Frank said.

"I'm gonna call you Charlie—OK?"

"Hey! My hair's not that long! It's not like I have a beard or something," Frank said.

"It's just a game silly, don't you wanna play with me, Charlie?" Red said, in a cutesy yet scolding tone.

"All right, I'm in, I'm Charlie. What should I call you?" he said.

"I think that's up to you, Charlie. It's only fair."

That made sense to him so he thought for a moment as they cruised down Route 202.

"Well, I guess in keeping with the Manson theme, I'll call you Sadie, and you Squeaky, since you haven't made a peep."

"Good names, Charlie. I say we celebrate our new names. Squeaky, light a joint. You wanna beer, Charlie?"

"Sure, it's about that time," Frank / Charlie said.

Squeaky with the blue hair passed him a coldish can of Narragansett.

"Breakfast is served."

Frank took a long swing of the lukewarm beer. He remembered hearing that his grandmother had hidden them in her sewing room back in the day.

"You don't say much do you, Squeaky?" Frank said.

Squeaky smiled back at him from the passenger seat and shook her head and passed the joint to Sadie.

"Squeaky's my bitch. She does anything I say. She doesn't like to talk, more like an action girl, you know. Play your cards right and maybe I'll make her blow you."

Frank laughed and Squeaky gave her a look that either said, "Oh, you're so bad!" or "You're a retard."

The Venom tape had ended and a Roky Erickson tape had gone in. They listened to the music from the alien and passed the joint around the car. There wasn't too much other traffic around. He was getting quite stoned.

"What are you up to today?" Frank asked. Then he added, "Roky speaks the truth. It is the night of the vampire."

"We're just out for a little horror show. You know, out for a drive. Got a couple of errands to do as well. Wanna come?"

"Usually." The marijuana had made him say that even though it was stupid, but it still produced more laughter. Hail hail THC.

"I always wanna come too. I am an orgasm addict. Driving always makes me so horny," Sadie said, and she slid one of her hands between her legs and started masturbating. This was easy for her to do in a miniskirt with no panties.

"You sure that's safe, Sadie?" Frank asked with a laugh. He could feel his cock hardening in his dirty jeans.

"Don't worry, I do this all the time, Chaaaaarlie," she moaned, her eyes rolling back as she stomped on the accelerator.

"That's fucking hot," he confided.

"Take out your thing," she demanded. The "thing" in question was about to burst out anyway and he was glad to oblige.

"Oh, yeah, it's big as a breadbox. Stroke it a little for me, yeah," she purred, while interrupting her fingering to adjust the rear view mirror.

"Now, Squeaky, get back there and give me a little show. Do it now Squeaky! I said NOW BITCH!"

Squeaky hopped over into the back seat. She wasted no time and slipped her bright red lipsticked lips around Frank's threatening erection. He noticed Cleopatra style black eyeliner on her as she began bobbing on his cock.

"And I thought you were just saying that to shock me," Frank said, and grinned.

"I never joke about dick sucking, Charlie. That's it. Hold her hair back for me, Charlie. She doesn't mind if you choke her a little. Yeah, that's it, baby. Shove it in there!" Sadie purred.

He leaned back and grinned. Weed and oral sex go together like cookies and milk. He tried his best to present it to Sadie in a dramatic fashion.

Sadie's body was heaving and spasming in response as the speedometer passed 80. They were going more than twenty-five over the speed limit—criminal speeding.

It felt good enough to be criminal to Frank as Squeaky worked him all the way down her throat. Frank's moaning harmonized with Sadie's soprano gasping as they approached a mutual climax, though he suspected she had had three or four from the sound of her jubilance.

"I'm gonna come!" he yelled, and Squeaky backed off until he was just barely between her bee sting lips and her hands worked their magic, stimulating Frank to shoot hard into her mouth. She gulped several times and it was done. Everything faded away for just a second.

She smiled up at him with only the thinnest line of dribble. The day WAS going well. He bummed a cigarette and they resumed their trip at a more legal speed.

"I think I'm in love with you, Sadie," Frank said, shattering the silence with a compliment to the director.

"Aw, can it with that corny shit, Charlie, you'll ruin the moment," Sadie said, but she said it sweetly.

"We're gonna grab a burger then go get some coke. Squeaky's never done coke before and I'm gonna get her fuuuucked up. You wanna play with us tonight, Charlie, and get fuuuuuucked up?" Sadie asked.

Frank found he no longer cared at all about waking up in a graveyard and having no idea how he got there. He felt like a new man, and fortune was smiling on his face.

"Yeah, I guess I could handle a little pick me up," he said.

"Well then, it must be destiny. First we need to fortify ourselves with burgers, because, like, we won't be able to eat for the rest of the night once the party really starts," Sadie said, her red hair taunting him.

The restaurant concept brought Frank back to earth. He reached into his back pocket and flipped out his wallet. He had thirty-seven dollars— more than good enough for burgers for all of them.

"Well, in appreciation for picking me up on the side of the road, and getting me high, and getting me off, I insist on purchasing these burgers for us three forthrightly, and maybe we can get more properly acquainted. Where do you wanna go, sexy Sadie?" he asked.

"Aw, thanks, Charlie, you are such a messiah. Now we don't have to dine and dash," Sadie said.

They giggled again. He was grateful he had the money because he was much too high to pull a stunt like that.

"For burgers in Augusta there's really only one place to go: Gregg Bob's All Steak Burger Emporium here we come," Sadie said.

"Isn't that the Armenian burger joint on Western Ave?" he said.

"I don't know, probably. There's some sort of funny flag in there and the employees wear festively colored weaved ponchos," said Sadie.

"Oh, yeah. My buddy always calls those drug rugs."

They laughed and drove and drank and smoked and then they were there. They lingered a little while at the petting zoo at the side of Gregg Bob's and the girls took turns petting a goat named Bealzabuddy.

After a while Frank was able to coax the girls away from the old goat and they walked into the adjoining restaurant. Within minutes they had what might have been a hot Greek waitress under a giant Day-Glo poncho taking their order of three cokes (no ice) and three Ultimate Gigantoramas.

The placemat propaganda promised them that the Gigantorama was the most awesome and oversized burger in the universe. It was irresistible.

"I love giant food," Sadie said.

"It is the American way."

Frank nodded in agreement with himself. None of them were able to finish the giant burgers. He doubted these young birds could get coke, but if they did, they would have full bellies.

Frank paid and they got back to the car bar in time for another coldish one. It was the last beer and they passed it around several times, but it didn't last. Squeaky started rolling another joint and they pulled out of the parking lot. These girls certainly liked to live it up, and that was OK with him. Frank was born a rambling man.

"Now we just gotta hit Cumby's for some more smokes and beer. Then we're gonna go see the candy man. I'm getting tired of driving. When we get there you take over Squeaky. Ugh, last time we went there, would you believe Squeaky stayed in the car and almost got abducted! I'm so glad you're here this time, you big strong man," Sadie said, and winked at Frank.

"Well, I can keep an eye on her, if you like," he volunteered, happy to be both useful and sedentary in his glazed condition.

"Cool, Charlie, I knew I could count on you to be cool. You're a real stand-up guy, you know that?" Sadie said. The joint went around a few times and then Squeaky put it out because they were at the convenience store. Every time she had passed the joint to him, he leaned forward and saw a black lacy bra peeking out from under Sadie's sliced up tiny black top and it lingered in his mind. There was red lettering on her shirt of a black metal band logo, but his vision was too blurry to quite make it out. Carpathian something-or-other. Frank was captivated by her.

Sadie had parked along the side of the Cumberland Farms convenience store. She left it running and went inside. Squeaky jumped out and hopped in the driver's seat. He noticed she was wearing fishnets and high heels under her 50's style polka dot dress. An anonymous teen girl had just sucked him off. *Sometimes hitchhiking worked out pretty good,* he thought. A smile crept up his face; she was hot!

The Misfits were speaking to him from the speakers and Frank was listening intently as he waited. Too much horror business driving late at night. He could relate to that shit. It was punk rock, and it was all he knew.

"So, Squeaky, are you the type that never ever talks or the type that just doesn't talk very often?" He waited a few moments before he got a reply.

"Neither, Charlie. I'm the type born with an inability to talk," Squeaky said.

"Ha, you're talking now. Good one," Frank said.

"You just think I'm talking to you. We are really communicating telepathically," she said.

"Well I guess that's certainly possible. I guess when you think about it all, communication is really telepathic."

"Tele-pathetic maybe."

Sadie burst out of the store wearing a Wonder Woman mask, a plastic bag in one hand and a six pack in the other. She scrambled into the car and Squeaky put the pedal to the floor. The car careened yodeling out of the parking lot with a high-pitched wail.

Frank kept a cool composure but inside his heart and mind were racing through the fog of beer and smoke. It was clear even in his current altered condition that he was an accessory to robbery now and he worried for a moment. Who cares, all the cops are chasing that serial strangler and have a lot bigger stuff to worry about. They hadn't been caught in the act and if no one was hurt, he doubted the cops would even investigate. Squeaky was flying down a flurry of back roads.

"Well, finally some cold beer! Give one up," Frank said. Sadie passed one back and he guzzled it down.

"So did we get enough scratch to get some coke or what?" Frank asked.

"Just a sec, let me see. Yeah, we got two hundred and ninety dollars, that's two fifty for an eight ball and that leaves us forty bucks for gas. Score."

"I never been part of a robbery before, that was kind of . . . sexually exciting," Frank said.

"Yeah, armed robbery always gets me wet. Crime is pleasure," Sadie said and licked her lips.

"I've had friends that did it before, but I never have," he said.

"Oh yeah, what did your friend do?" Sadie asked.

"Are you a cop?" he said. She laughed.

"Come on, professional curiosity. Do tell," Sadie pried.

"OK, settle down. I'll tell you because it's a funny story actually. A friend of mine lived down south and worked at this Dunkin Donuts down there. He came up here to Maine to visit and brought his uniform with him. One day while he was here he went to the Dunkin Donuts on Western Ave and said he was the new guy. They said OK and showed him what to do for a few minutes then left him alone out front. He grabbed a couple of boxes of doughnuts and the money from the register and walked out. He only got like 70 bucks, but he never got caught," Frank said.

"That is funny. That's a good idea," she said.

"Do you have a gun?"

"Such personal questions, Charlie. Don't you know it isn't polite to ask a lady that?" she replied.

"Hey, it's cool, be mysterious Sadie."

"If you're a good boy maybe I'll let you hold it later."

They drove on in silence through the woods until they came to a cabin on a lake. Again Frank and Squeaky were directed to wait in the car while Sadie went in and took care of business.

Time seemed to stand still. Squeaky shared a smoke with him. She put a Ramones tape in. Ten songs later Sadie was back and she was grinding her teeth, with wild eyes.

Frank laughed when he saw her.

"We happy Sadie?" he said.

"We're happy, Charlie. The football is not empty." She laughed.

"Fire Walk with me. I just watched that flick, that's wild. Later that night the friend I watched it with was killed in front of me by a terrible wolfman. It bit his fucking head off; it was a real horror show."

"Are you serious?"

"Like a clown with a hard on."

"EW . . . that is a terrible thought."

They were driving to Squeaky's house. Her parents were out of town. She lived in Windsor in a farmhouse that was a few miles outside Augusta.

Frank was glad to stretch his legs after being confined in the small auto. They were finally at Squeaky's parents' picturesque two-story farmhouse. It was a nice and isolated place. There were only five houses on the road. The kind of place where you could do pretty much anything you wanted without attracting too much attention. He dug these digs.

They went inside and sat on the couch. Squeaky put a Danzig record on while Sadie chopped up big lines of cocaine for them on a glass coffin shaped coffee table. Danzig crooned out his Devil hymns over dark electric blues metal. Sadie produced a candy striped glass tube and they all blew the lines. Two rails for each of them, one for each nostril. It was pretty good stuff and it hit fast. Soon they were all fast talkers and laughing and drinking beer.

Frank felt as if he owned the world.

"Hail Satan!" he shouted, overcome with gratitude.

"Hail Satan!" the two girls cried in unison and perfect ecstasy. They must be reading his mind. This was hardly surprising because Frank had found in the past excessive drug use and sexual activity broke down these boundaries.

"Oh, Charlie, do you really love the Devil, or are you just trying to be cool?"

"It's probably me that should be asking you little girls that question. Why, I bet I was worshiping the devil when the closest you could get to it was finger painting," he said.

"Yeah, well maybe you've been doing it longer, but we're serious about it, Charlie, and we're not alone," Sadie said.

"No one's alone. How old are you girls?" he asked.

"We're old enough. How old are you Charlie?"

"I'm old enough too," Frank said, with a hungry smile.

"Little late for that bullshit isn't it, Charlie?" Squeaky had turned off the regular light and turned on a red light. They did more coke. Squeaky put on a Mayhem record. The insane speed of the drums put them in a dark evil cocaine trance.

"I feel like I've known you two a lot longer than just tonight. I don't believe in coincidence. This is not random chance; this is destiny. This is synchronicity."

"That's the way it always feels," Squeaky said.

"Don't say too much Squeaky. We must be careful," Sadie said.

"You doubt me? You don't trust me?" he said.

"We just met you, we have to be careful," Sadie said.

He was not pleased by their lack of faith in him and the coke was making him feel as if he could do anything.

"You think you're more hardcore than me? You're not. I'm up for anything," he said. The black metal was getting his dander up.

"Don't take it so personally, GG Allin. We did just meet you," Squeaky said.

"Yeah, look at how the Norwegian metal scene used to be. Now those guys were hardcore. Burning fucking churches down and killing people, musicians don't get more hardcore than that," Sadie said.

"I agree we should all aspire to such diligence," he said.

"All right, then, I dare you to burn down a church," Sadie said. Frank thought about it a second. He felt that the churches should be burned down. What would Euronymous do?

"You're really asking me to burn down a church, you mean like tonight?" he said, pondering it.

"Tonight's the only night, Charlie. If you burn down a church, I'll even let you fuck Squeaky in the ass," Sadie added. Frank looked over to Squeaky.

Squeaky looked him dead in the eyes and said, "If you burn down a church you can totally fuck me in the ass."

"Why the fuck not. Let's get wild. Let's get loose. One church? Shit, we should go around and burn down every one in town. Now, that would send a message."

"Get serious, gasoline ain't cheap. Let's stick with one for tonight. We can always go out again. Are you really in?"

"I'm in. You know I'm in. I was born to be in and out and in and out and in and out of your fucking ass. But I'm saying right now, I'm doing it because it's something I've always wanted to do. I am not doing this just so I can fuck Squeaky in the ass, even though after I burn that fucker down, I will fuck that ass, and fuck it promptly, and fuck it hard. YEAH! ALRIGHT!"

They did another line and went into the garage for supplies. He found what he was looking for—a full gas can next to the family lawn mower.

"Must be fate, must be fate," he sang, gakked into oblivion. He grabbed the can and loaded it into the car while managing to jump high and double click his heels together.

"Hey, don't spill," Sadie said.

"I know, I know I'm good. Just a little excited you know."

Squeaky laughed and rolled a couple more joints, liberally lacing them with coke. They got back in the car and started driving. They smoked and drove for about an hour before they started really looking for a suitable target.

They eventually found their church in the middle of nowhere. They parked in front of it and waited for five minutes. No cars drove by on the main road. It was up a winding driveway as well, so it seemed an ideal place. They did another line in the car off a small mirror Sadie had in her purse. Frank started shaking the can and squirting the gasoline onto the front of the church. Sadie climbed on top of the hood of the car and spread her legs wide, her right hand busy in a now familiar dance.

Frank was feeling strangely confident as he spilled the last of the gasoline away in a trail from the church. He felt a certain strength channeling up through him.

"In the name of Satan, burn motherfucker burn!" Frank screamed. His whole body was shaking with rage as he touched the gas with his Zippo lighter.

It looked so beautiful. The line of fire raced to the building and the big white church was engulfed in flames fast. They stood there and watched it for what seemed like an hour, but they knew it was really only a couple minutes, then they hopped back in car. They drove away very fast and never heard any sirens. They drove around the back roads and a couple of hours later found themselves back at Squeaky's folk's house as the sun was coming up.

"I never came as hard in my life as I did watching you light that church on fire, Charlie. You are something special. You are our brother," Sadie said.

"Why, thank you, Sadie. I'm not sure exactly what the future has in store for us, girls, but I promise you one thing, it will be interesting," he said. They laughed.

"So, Squeaky, what do you think of coke?" Sadie asked.

"I like it. It makes me ready to kill," she answered.

"You got something else coming I don't know if you're gonna like," Frank said, and the girls laughed again.

"I can take it I'm tough," Squeaky said.

"I'm watching," Sadie said.

"I don't think I could perform without you."

Frank went into the bathroom to look for something to use for lube. All he could find was a bottle of hand lotion. He decided it was good enough and brought it back out into the living room.

"We are brought together by the burning of the church and now we are connected by fire. We can use our real names. My real name is Mildred, and my birth name is Anne McGoldstein," his new friend formerly known as Sadie said.

"I'm Trish," Squeaky said.

"Frank."

"And now we all know each other," Mildred said.

"Good let's fuck. All this crime and drugs has given me a raging hard on."

Trish stripped off her dress leaving her in a black lace garter belt and stockings. She wasn't wearing any other underwear. As usual Mildred was playing with herself on the couch.

"Come on its, muffin eating time, Trishy," Mildred said, giggling.

Trish crawled forward on all fours and dug in, presenting her ass to him in the process as a bonus. He dipped a finger into the coke on the table and worked it inside to numb her. Mildred was moaning and staring at Frank as he dropped his pants and rubbed hand lotion all over his cock with one hand. He worked a middle finger up Trish's secret temple with the other. He looked down and saw Mildred's happy face and the back of Trish's head buried in between her thighs. He kept looking down, and seeing that beautiful all seeing eye looking back at him made him feel harder than ever before. It was the right time and the right place.

He placed his battering ram at the gates and pushed and felt the expected resistance as Trish's body tensed up and she pressed forward and gasped. It was a tight velvet heaven. He stroked her hair to sooth her and laid there impaling her, letting her get accustomed to its girth and depth. It was the most erotic moment of Frank's life. It was the way she pushed back on it. The way she cutely bit her lip and slammed it home with a violence that surprised them both. He was completely overcome with lust. He started to fuck her faster and harder. Trish was too involved in the sodomy to be licking Mildred at this pace, so Mildred was fingering herself in Trish's face as Frank sodomized her. It was too tight and perfect for Frank to last too long. Mildred was making these over dramatized porno-style faces at him, and for some reason it was really getting under his skin. He screamed out his orgasm, and pulled out, lassoing both of them with white rope. It was the best of times, it was the best of times.

Chapter 4
The Wolf Diaries: 3 weeks prior

Josh was walking alone in the woods near Moosehead Lake, trying to get away and clear his head, when he was chosen. He was on a camping trip with his family and they were driving him crazy. Plus it was October, which is not the best time for camping unless you love a good chill. Josh did not.

He went off on his own in hope of killing some squirrels with a slingshot to vent frustration. He was in a devilish mood. *If I had an ax instead of this slingshot, I swear I would ax murder my family,* he thought, and began to fantasize while he walked between the looming pines.

Josh pictured himself running back to the campsite. In his daydream, he found his father on his knees, trying to light the campfire, and swung his booted foot up, connecting hard with his father's face, knocking him onto his back.

"Fuck you, Dad, you get some fucking firewood, you fat lazy cunt!" he cried as he swung the ax down into the center of his father's chest, splitting him open like a blood-filled flesh balloon. This attracted the attention of his mother and sister who scrambled out of the tent.

"You know I hate the C word you little asshole!" his mother cried, not realizing the serious nature of the situation yet. She managed to say this just in time to be decapitated in one mighty blow from Josh's ax.

Her head flew through the air before landing in the fire that had just started to catch. His little sister started screaming and Josh swung the ax with precision, severing her tongue from her mouth. It flew from her mouth and landed in a bird's nest in a nearby tree, waking up a family of baby birds, so blood poured both out of the bird's nest and her mouth. She ran off into the woods and Josh let her go. It wasn't like she could ever tell anyone what happened. She would most likely go off and join a bear family or something.

Josh was knocked from this fantastical reverie when he stumbled onto something even more bizarre; two huge monster wolves fucking! He stood a mere eight feet from them with his mouth gaping open at the two giant black man-sized wolf creatures with glowing pink eyes.

Josh was so alarmed by the sudden appearance of the behemoths that he fired the sling shot. It must have been fate or shit luck; the ball bearing flew with precision and slipped through the male wolf's right eye coming to rest deep in the wolf's brain. His lifeless body pitched backward and it caused a great slurping sound as his cock ripped out of the she-wolf.

Half a breath later the bitch was on top of Josh's chest, pinning him to the ground, his slingshot knocked into the underbrush.

Josh was certain he was done for. He lay on the ground terrified, staring up into the all-consuming eyes of the beast. Drool was starting to drip from her mouth and her face came closer and licked his cheek. She bared her teeth and spoke.

"Take off your pants!" she barked.

Josh just stood there.

"Now!" she demanded, slicing through his leather belt with a swipe of one giant paw.

"Wh-wh-what?" Josh tried, his eyes working faster than his brain.

"You interrupted something I needed, and now you have to finish me off or I will kill you as you deserve, manling," the wolf hissed.

She licked his neck again and it gave him goose bumps. She got off his chest and assumed the position. Josh knew if he tried to run he would be killed. He let his pants fall to the ground, thinking he'd probably be too scared to be able to get a hard-on.

She leaned her head around and her long pink tongue came out and lapped several times across his dick and balls. He was disgusted, but there was something in the saliva that made him hard as a rock. He looked forward at the wolf pussy presented in front of him.

There was a yellowish fluid dripping from it and he closed his eyes and thrust deep inside the bitch's fiery hole. The wolf slammed back into him and they fucked, and the longer they did it, the less awkward it felt and the better it was until he exploded in her. He tried to pull out afterward, but found he could not as the base of his cock had become swollen and he could not withdraw. They lay on the ground together until he could feel himself getting hard again inside her and they fucked again. Four times later he was able to get his cock out of her. She ran off without another word.

Josh didn't really know what to think, but he put his pants back on, throwing aside his ruined belt. He looked over at the body of the male wolf on the forest floor and shook his head.

He went back to his family and the rest of the camping trip went on without event.

For about a week everything was normal. Josh was even sort of starting to forget it ever happened. He didn't tell anyone about it.

Josh had just about managed to forget it when his sense of smell started to go crazy. His nose grew so sensitive he was able to tell when family members came and went in the house. He craved meat all the time.

It was hard to get used to. There were a lot of gross smells out there and he was now aware of them all. He had heard in school that the sense of smell was just an extension of the sense of taste and the thought that he was tasting all of these gross disgusting things revolted him at first. Also improving was his night vision, and if it got any better he thought he would be able to see in the dark.

I guess there are worse things in the world than wolf pussy, he thought, sitting alone in his room. Then the hunger started coming to him and it hit him hard. He would masturbate for hours, but he never seemed to be fulfilled, and when he would climax it would come out with such forceful abundance it would splatter the ceiling, and his cock would stay hard and demand further abuse. He found himself fantasizing about that encounter in the woods. He would see those feral wolf eyes in his dreams glowing above him as he came.

Josh woke up from one such dream and was still able to feel her feet against his chest holding him against the ground, and feel the bitch's hot breath against his neck. He grunted in frustration. Why do I always wake up before the good part!

His sister Tess ran in from across the hall. She barged in without knocking from the adjoining bedroom, and Josh threw the blanket over his throbbing erection.

"Brother, are you okay? I heard you screaming," Tess said, bursting in laughing. Her white blonde shoulder length hair tumbled down onto a skin-tight ripped up black pirate flag shirt. The shirt closely gripped her training bra, which peeked out from the holes.

"What did I tell you about knocking? I told you next time you busted in without knocking, I was going to rape you."

"Go ahead, I'll tell Mom."

"You're such a tattle tale. I would rape you, but you'd like it too much, you dirty fucking whore," Josh said, trying to sound harsh.

"Brother, don't be such a gross guy. Smoke a bowl with me," Tess said.

"Yeah, okay, Tess, but you're fucking packing it."

She got out the skull head bong and packed it full of weed she had stolen from their mom. She sat down on the bed with her brother/best friend and they got stoned. They had a love hate relationship and fought a lot, but were always together.

"You shouldn't be around me, Tess. I don't know how long I can control myself. I need some pussy. You gotta help me. Can I trust you, Tess?" Josh said.

"Yeah, brother, don't be stupid. You know you can trust me, but you can't do it with me," she said.

"Yeah, you wish I'd do it with you. No, this isn't about that. I mean, can I really trust you. You cannot tell anyone this, you understand me? This is just between me and you. None of your little friends, no one."

"Okay, sure."

"Well when we went camping, I fucked a wolf, and now something's happening to me. I'm horny all the time and I can smell everything. I can even smell your stinky pussy right now through your cut offs."

"Anyone could smell that. I haven't changed my underwear for a week, so there! I'm a gross girl," she said, and laughed.

"All kidding aside, sis, wash your nasty gash, all right? It's basic feminine hygiene. I can also kinda see in the dark."

"Wow that's so cool, brother. That's so awesome. You are totally turning into a werewolf. I will be the most popular girl in junior high. You can eat my teachers. They will have to give me good grades or else. You should turn me into a werewolf too, and then we can kill Mom and Dad and take over the house. Then Captain Planet could be my boyfriend, and we could live together in Mom's room," she gushed.

"Not so fast, Tess, you must first do something for me to prove your loyalty, before I would even consider making you a werewolf. Plus there's no way in hell you would get mom's room. Don't forget who's king daddy werewolf, Tess. I am. It's me. I'm king daddy werewolf. I fucked the wolf. How many wolves did you fuck, huh?" he said.

"I didn't fuck any wolves, brother, you know that."

"That's right, so you listen to me when I speak. Are you ready to help me? Will you do what I want?"

"Anything, brother," Tess breathed.

"Good, that is the way you should treat your brother. Now first things first. My cock is demanding action. I need some pussy bad, so you gotta go out and convince one of your little friends to come back here and fuck me. Can you do this?"

"I don't know, brother. I guess I can try. Mary's a slut," she said, after thinking about it.

"Then go do it."

Tess was gone about an hour before she returned with Mama. Mama was her girlfriend Mary's mother. She was a lonely older red haired lady who would buy the kids alcohol and smoke weed with them. She was thirty-seven years old and about twenty-seven pounds overweight. She was an alcoholic and you could get her to do just about anything. Some people said she was a little retarded, but Josh and Tess just thought she was young at heart.

"Get out of here, Tess, you can listen if you want," Josh said, dismissing his sister. Tess flipped him off and left the room.

"Hey Josh," Mama said.

"Hey, Mama, how's it going?" Josh said.

"It's going pretty good, Josh. How's it going with you?" she said, taking a swig off a bottle of cheap wine.

"It's going pretty good for me. Things are looking up."

"I see they are," she said, eyeing the large bulge the sheet was barely covering and stumbling across the room. Josh took her face in his hands and licked her cheek.

"You know, Josh, it's dangerous for guys your age to get so backed up."

"Is it?" he said.

47

"Yeah, it can cause cancer. You'd better let me help you with that," she said, reaching over and grabbing his cock through the sheet. She gasped at the size of it.

"You want me to help you work out this muscle?" she said.

"I do," he said, pulling the sheet back, exposing his muscular body and erection. She bent down and took him in her mouth.

"Close your eyes and I will do something special for you," she said, and he obliged her.

She took out her dentures and placed them on the table beside the bed and really started to work on him. He let out a quick moan. He motioned for her to take down her sweat pants and she did without skipping a beat. He lifted her up and swung her around so he could lick the tangy spot between her legs.

She had little pieces of toilet paper stuck to her privates but he didn't care, he was a wolf fucker. He flipped her over and thrust himself upon her and they fucked loud and messy for a long time. After he had fucked her senseless, Josh asked her to bring him some beer. She said she would and left.

He felt himself growing stronger every day, more in tune with the primal black chaos of nature. He was aware of the moon at all times and he knew that in three days it would be full for the first time since the camping trip, and he knew something big was going to happen.

Tess returned from the store with two Scary Larry's energy drinks. She had purchased them with the food stamp card her mother left her before leaving for the evening.

"Brother, play video games with me. Please!" she begged.

He complied and they started playing a game where they were able to make a strange techno sounding song, and then Mama dropped off the beer.

"I am the wicked king Wicker," Josh said.

"Then I'm princess Wicker," Tess chimed in.

"Mama is my slave and she is just the first of many."

"Oh, brother, can't we kill our parents tonight. They are so annoying. I swear they are conspiring to get on my nerves, and I can't take it!"

"It's not time yet, Tess, but it might be soon, so be ready."

"I'm gonna stab Mom, gonna stab her up. I bet I cum when I stick that miserable bitch," she said.

"You don't even know what you're talking about. You never came," Josh said.

"Yeah, I did once. I made Amy lick me. I said she couldn't spend the night unless she did it. It didn't take too much convincing. Girls are dumb. It was nice, though. I watched cartoons while she did it," Tess said.

"Good for you and Captain fuckin' Planet. That's what you should be doing at your age. You are too young to be fucking guys. If I find out you are, I will kill them and punish you!"

"Don't worry, brother. Guys are gross."

"How were the streets tonight?"

"They were pretty empty because everyone's afraid of the Strangler."

"I thought he only struck on the 11th of every month."

"Lately he's been branching out. Even slashed a few throats. So far the score is Sand Hillside Strangler 27, APD 0."

"Well, I don't have anything against the guy. I don't even know him. Who knows, maybe he's some kind of wolf creature like me. All I know is this town is going crazy. Even a big daddy werewolf like me doesn't feel safe."

Chapter 5
The Secret Lives of Teenage Girls

It was six thirty Monday morning and Mildred wished she was back in her cozy bed under the covers. She stood shivering in the cold dark blackness waiting for Trish to come and pick her up for high school.

She was wearing skintight black jeans and a pea coat, her bright red hair concealed under a furry Russian style hat. She would have skipped but she had already missed five days this month and knew she couldn't get away with pushing her luck much more. The cold was getting to her and she was trembling in her size five combat boots. *This is bullshit, I should just drop out,* she thought.

Trish pulled up and Mildred got in her car.

"Hey, Millie," Trish said, her blue black hair peeking out from under a purple beret.

"Jesus fucking cold Christ, turn on the heat it's freezing in here," Millie said.

"Sorry, it should heat up in a second. Here, this will take the edge off," Trish said, and passed Mildred a joint. She was wearing black gloves with the fingers cut out, and her nails were painted bright red.

"I need this fucking thing just to keep warm. Any news on my man?" Millie said, firing it up.

"If you're talking about my man, The Sand Hillside Strangler, I'm afraid there is no news. The city was safe because he just couldn't tear himself away from ravishing me."

"You're lucky I know you're lying, sister," she said, laughing. "I know you're lying because he was with me all night. It was this sweet piece that kept the city safe last night." She gave a tap to her plush posterior for emphasis. This was a familiar game on the boring days when there weren't any new headlines for the killer.

"I know more about him than you do," Trish bragged.

"Oh yeah, well then how many people has he killed?"

"He has killed twenty seven people in the last 18 months confirmed, with another three missing persons suspected, just not found yet," Trish said.

"Well, that was an easy one. Anyone could have gotten that one. Here's one for the true fan. How many were strangled?" Millie said.

"Um, that's a hard one. The first nine and then the last two?" Trish said.

"Ha, I win. I am best. No, it was the first seven that were strangled, then our Maine man began to experiment a little and he came back to his tried and true method on victims eleven, fifteen through seventeen, and on twenty-six," Millie said.

"How come you can know all that stuff and still not pass all your classes?"

"Duh-uh, because school is boring bullshit."

"My Dad told me in his day they never had any serial killers in Augusta, but now there's always at least one everywhere you go. He said killings like that were very rare flukes," Trish said.

"We live in illuminated times," Millie said.

"Yeah, we'll be able to stop going to school soon enough. Daddy says it would look bad if we stop going to school right now. Like we might know stuff we shouldn't. He says something big is coming, though."

"Yeah, like the end of the world."

"I don't think that's what he meant. I think he was referring to something everyone doesn't already know. Something that is supposed to happen first, maybe. This weekend was really wild. Are you worried we're gonna get in trouble? I was a little scared at first, but I'm mostly over it now," Trish said.

"There's no use being paranoid, hon. We're young, sexy teenage girls. We can do anything we want. Besides, they'll probably just blame it on ol' Sandy," Millie said.

"I don't think he would like it if he knew you called him that," Trish said.

"Oh no, he loves it," Millie said.

They were now in the parking lot of Fony High School. They each ate a stick of gum and put perfume on before going to class, to cover up the marijuana scent.

The day was frightening in its normality. Most of the teachers ignored the two girls and the ones that didn't just tried to look down their shirts.

The teachers were too afraid of the students to put up too much of hassle about anything.

The best part of the day was lunch, not because of the disgusting cafeteria food, no some things never change. It was the only time that they could hang out and converse unrestrained.

They always sat at a certain table in the back. Everyone knew it was theirs and no one else would try and sit there. Mildred was the first one there and then Trish. They had both brought lunches consisting of a can of Mountain Dew and a candy bar. Mildred had a heath bar while Trish had a Snickers. The hexagonal lunch tables sat six people comfortably. The next person to show up was Josh. He was a short muscular crazy person. The girls liked him, and the teachers didn't know what to do with him. He was a weirdo who had been left back a few times.

"Hey, Josh, you've been weirder than normal lately. Why?" Mildred asked.

Josh just barked in reply and started humping the table.

The rest of the school day passed in a blur for the girls. After school they were glad to reconvene at Trish's house. They were out of fresh pot and had to break into Trish's roach bottle.

It was a wine bottle about half full of very resonated roaches. They only smoked from it in times of dire need and desperation. Trish packed a bright red plastic bong full of the harsh second-generation weed. Millie put "Free Cocaine" by The Dwarves on the turntable.

"Saturday night was real wild, but it's my turn and I got something REALLY hot lined up for tomorrow," Trish said bopping to the frenzied beat.

"Hey, my game was hot, you bitch! I had you suck a stranger's cock without even saying a word to him, and he was fucking hot. It wasn't some nasty old dude or something. I'm getting wet just thinking of you with that hot rod in your mouth, but turnabout is fair play. You played my game and I'll play yours," Mildred hissed back.

"You need to be on both sides of the spectrum or you'll never get an accurate picture," Trish said.

"Oh, baby, when you talk smart like that you make me so wet," Millie said.

"Fuck off. I think it's gonna work out with Frank. What are the odds we'd find someone like that while playing the game," Trish said.

"It's truly a gift from Wodan," Millie said.

"He's perfect, I can't believe there was someone like that operating in this area and we didn't already know him. This means something I don't understand. Ron is going to be very pleased. This is good news for everyone. That reminds me I should call my parents and check in. They should be back in a couple days," Trish said.

"I miss them. You have the coolest parents. I would totally fuck your Dad," Millie said.

"No shit, slut, too bad he wouldn't fuck you!" Trish said.

"Well, there's a war going on, it's not like a man in his position can just spend all day screwing his admirers. Though I wouldn't be surprised if he penciled me in soon enough," Millie said.

"There's always been a war going on. Face it, Millie, my Dad's just not into young stuff. Maybe when you get a little older you can wreck my home," Trish said.

"I'll just have to settle for being the adopted daughter, I guess," Millie said.

"I'm gonna go call them. You can watch TV or whatever," Trish said.

"Okay, I'll just stay here and try to get high enough to eat you out, bitch," Mildred said.

"Yeah, right, I know you. You'll be begging for a taste by the time I get back. C'mon, please, please just let me lick it a little. I got the cunt munchies! Please, please! You can watch TV or something. You won't even know I'm down there. Please, please, please, I'm bored. C'mon, just for a couple minutes. If you don't like it I'll stop, I promise," Trish said, mocking her.

"What can I say? That devil weed makes me a pervert," Millie said, her pale white cheeks flushing a deep red.

"I wouldn't have you any other way, Mill, Mill. You've really turned me into a perv as well, with this game of yours. Like . . . it's all I think about these days. Nothing else quite flips my switch anymore, you know?" Trish said.

"I feel the same way. Whenever I masturbate I'm always thinking of old games or dreaming up what to do for the next one."

Trish left to use the telephone and Mildred took a monster bong hit. Mildred flipped on the TV and turned it to the local news to check for killer updates. People were getting so disturbed by the all the freak disasters that the news was focusing on crime a lot more to distract them. That was just fine for Trish, who, like most people, was held enthralled by the true crime stories.

The Sand Hillside Strangler was by far the most brutal and out of control serial killer ever in Augusta, probably ever in Maine, but he was not national news yet. There was a retrospective special on, consisting of interviews with various victim's families, however, it did not hold Mildred's attention, as she had seen it several times before, and had all the good lines down pat.

Trish burst in through the door shrieking and jumping up and down.

"Daddy was so pleased when I told him about the church burning that he said he'd buy us IPhones!" she shrieked. The girls clutched on to each other and jumped up and down on the bed. Then they celebrated with a frenzied sixty-nine.

They weren't lesbians in a strict sense, they were just satisfying a mutual itch. To them it was just masturbation, only better because you had help. It was advanced masturbation. It didn't get them off like the game did, but it made everyday hormonal teenage life possible.

They lay huddled together, smoking on Trish's big pink bed. Trish was the first to break the silence.

"Is today one of those annoying nights when you have to go home?" she asked.

"Nah. I told them I was staying over tonight," Mildred said.

"Sweet, cause we got work to do. Daddy said we had to hit another store tonight or Thursday. This one is in Waterville," Trish said.

"Did he ask what you spent the money on?" Millie asked.

"Yeah, I said we spent the day at the spa getting massages and manicures," Trish said.

"Good one. Of course, now I want to go to the spa," Millie said.

"We'll go soon."

"Kiss kiss. Why do you think we're robbing these stores?"

"Who knows? It's supposed to be part of a larger plan, and we're on a need to know basis, but it's hard to say. Sometimes I wonder if it's just a test of what we're capable of. But he's really specific about what should be done so, who knows maybe there is some sort of grand design," Trish said.

"Well maybe we'll know eventually. I'm just glad we're finally allowed to participate," Millie said.

They jumped in the shower together and then dressed for battle. They had a gram and a half of coke left over and they broke into that, and hit 95 North to Waterville. Trish popped an Accused tape in and grinding their teeth they were good to go.

"The weirdest thing about my phone call with Daddy was that he didn't seem surprised at all about Frank, just excited, and you know Daddy, he keeps his cool. He was surprised about the church, but it seemed almost as if he expected that we were going to find someone new," Trish said.

"That's weird, but he always knows everything," Millie said.

"He's a well-connected Daddy. Oh yeah, he said to say he was proud of you for pulling off the last store by yourself and we should both do this one," Trish added.

They were both wearing bulky baggy clothes to try and conceal their gender, but it wasn't very effective because they were both petite girls. Trish was 5'2 and Mildred was only two inches taller. Trish's flamboyant hair was concealed under a black woolen cap. They each were armed with a Walther PPK pistol and a bowie knife in a boot holster for back up. The guns were gifts from Trish's dad.

They had to drive around for a while before they found the right store. Mildred spotted it and they pulled in. Trish was glad they'd made it in their time window otherwise they would have gotten a lot less money. Her father had told her when the night drops happened.

There was one other car already there, so they pulled up to the gas pump and filled it up. They parked on the far side so they were obscured from view. They were able to dawdle at the pump long enough for the other customer to leave.

It was action time. The girls rolled in old school with nylon stockings over their faces. The obese clerk didn't know what to make of them when they walked through the door.

"Is this some kind of joke?" he asked, startled.

"This is not a joke. This is a fucking robbery! Put your hands over your head and this will be over in a minute," Trish said. She opened her coat to show him the gun holstered to her waist. Mildred went to the back of the store and drew her gun, covering the entrance and pacing back and forth. The clerk raised his hands.

"Y'all seem like nice girls. Are you sure this is what y'all want to be doing? I mean, it's not too late to call this whole thing off. You girls have your whole lives ahead of you. I wouldn't tattle on you or nothing. I promise," he said.

"No more talking out of you. Here's what I want you to do. With one hand pick up a paper bag and hold it up high. Now with the other hand open the register and put the money in the bag. It is a simple task that you can do fast, follow these instructions now and you will not be hurt, and we will be gone. What do you care anyway right, I can't imagine they are buying your loyalty in this shit hole," Trish said.

The clerk followed her instructions. The door opened and in walked a burly bearded giant of a man. He was wearing a giant pair of blue denim overalls and a giant NASCAR t-shirt the size of a circus tent. That's when the robbery got out of hand, and the whole night went crazy.

Chapter 6
Frankie Goes to the Grave

Frank sat on his bed in his apartment. He was still trying to wrap his mind around the events of the last couple of days. If he was going to come to terms with it he would need some help. He also, much to his chagrin, would need to leave his room.

He walked out through the computer room into the living room. Dan, one of Frank's two roommates, sat in front of one of the computer stations. He had long brown hair tied in a ponytail and a mustache. The computer room had three computers in it and the walls were lined with strange books.

Dan was watching Gilmore Girls on the computer while eating a big bowl of Ramen noodles with a can of mixed vegetables added in.

Nayte burst in, returning from work. He was wearing a red golf shirt untucked from khaki work slacks. He was half Indian and had the sides and back of his head shaved. His face was clean-shaven except for a scruffy patchy neck beard. He was the second roommate.

Nayte worked at a video store. Dan fixed computers, among other things, for a living and Frank was currently milking unemployment.

"Guess what, Frankie!" Nayte exclaimed. His face was a huge smile.

"What's that?" Frank said.

"I just bought an eighth and you and me are gonna smoke the whole thing tonight!" Nayte yelled.

Dan didn't smoked weed. He didn't need too. He was already somewhere else. Frank had met him through Nayte. Dan and Nayte had been friends since childhood.

Dan was drinking an ever-present glass of wine he would fill from the box in the fridge and chain smoking. These were people Frank trusted and he felt he could tell them anything.

"I burned down a church with these girls last night, I was in this cocaine ecstasy, it was real wild," Frank blurted out.

"That was you that burned down Saint Bobbies? I knew it must have been someone I knew that did that as soon I heard about it. That was a really stupid move, man. Do you wanna go to jail or something?" Dan said.

"I don't care, fuck it. If that guy can kill 27 people and get away with it, I think I'll be OK. I always wanted to burn down a church and I guess the timing was just right. If I get caught, I get caught. No big deal. I don't think I will, though."

"Arson is a hard crime to get caught for. You'll probably be all right. I'll pull in some favors and check to see if the local authorities have any leads. Just play it cool and go about things as usual," Dan said.

"You burned down your first church, hurray! Let's celebrate!" Nayte said in a high-pitched voice that sped up and slowed down. They celebrated with bong hits.

"You look pale as fuck, dude," Nayte said, staring at Frank intently.

"It's true you do kinda look like shit," Dan confirmed.

"Maybe you need a large dose of cough medicine? A really large dose," Nayte suggested.

"I'll get better, I think I'm going to go take a constitutional. Get some fresh air. I'll check you guys a little later on." Nervous all of a sudden, Frank walked to the front door.

Next to the door was a bookshelf with Crowley's Thoth Tarot deck on it. It was his habit to always cut the cards before leaving the house, at least when cows weren't waiting out front. He cut the six of cups. It represented pleasure and the commencement of increase. He smiled and walked out the door.

It was an hour after sunset and there was a big orange moon in the sky. It was so beautiful Frank could not help but stare as he walked along the train tracks behind his house.

Far from feeling like shit, he felt great. He felt even better outside in the cool night air. He felt comforted and empowered by the dark. He felt aware of everything that lay under its blanket. Nothing was hidden from him, nothing could hide from him. He tripped over a big root but caught himself just shy of getting a face full of dirt. Well, almost nothing could hide from him.

He crept along the trail until he came to the graveyard that lay beyond Bolley's Famous Franks. He thought of all his delicious times there.

He felt pulled toward the graveyard by an unyielding force and it pulled him from his dog dreams. He had hung out in graveyards hundreds of times and always felt at home among the dead, but this was different. It was like nothing he had every felt before.

Frank slipped into the boneyard and heard a whispering emanating from the graves. He could hear them, and it came on at first like a sort of a white noise, of them all together, but then as he focused in he could hear the melodies of the individual voices. This was something that had never happened to him before.

Once he heard the voices he knew beyond the shadow of doubt that they had always been there, and it was him that had changed. It felt like déjà vu, or waking up. He reached out and grabbed onto a tombstone to keep from falling over.

He was drawn to a particular grave, it was an old one. There was a high-pitched childish voice singing up from the earth, in front of the old slate stone. It was a mournful lament that he could not quite make out the words to. He thought it was in French, perhaps.

He looked at the small rectangular gravestone. It read "Here lies Josette Poulin Bloved Daughter 1898–1906." The engraver had started to run out of room by the end of the last word and the last four letters of daughter went straight up. She'd been eight years old.

"Hello can you hear me?" Frank called down to her grave, feeling foolish.

"You're the new mister, who are you? I haven't seen you before."

It was eerie hearing this high-pitched child's voice coming from nowhere, but he wasn't frightened. Still the giggling was creepy.

"My name is Frank. Who are you?" Frank said.

"My name is Josette, but you know that," the ghost said.

"I can barely hear you. Can you come closer to me," he said.

"I sure can, Frank, for you. You are special," Josette said.

A glowing little girl floated up from the grave. She was wearing a frilly frock and he stumbled back in shock. He wondered if seeing the werewolf had awakened something in him.

"It's good to be out of the endless black, Frank. Thank you." She smiled at him and curtsied.

"Well. you are just about the most adorable ghost I have ever seen. Thanks for showing up." She smiled at that and he swore he saw a quick flash of color on her translucent cheeks.

"I was sent to you, and you called me Frank. I've been in the in-between space. I am here for you now," Josette said.

"Hey, I'm just a regular guy looking for a good time in a graveyard, but if you wanna tag along

66

who am I to say no. Besides I could use the company," Frank said.

"You're anything but regular, Frank. In fact, you have a new friend who has sent me here to help you," she said.

"What are you talking about?" Frank asked the spirit.

"It's not that easy, Frank. The end of the world is coming and you've been chosen to help. What do you think, Frank?"

"What do I have to do? What's the catch here? Am I some kind of slave?"

"No, Frank. That's not the way it works. There is both a clockwork precision and a complete chaos."

"Sure, I'm in."

"I'm here to help you, Frank."

"Welcome onboard, Josette. Try to keep me alive if you can."

"Your life is worthless. You are just getting to the good part, Frank. The story of your death and resurrection. Come, let's leave this graveyard. It's been a long time for me," Josette said.

He didn't mind and he started the walk back to the house. Josette floated along beside him.

When he looked at her she sort of flickered like an old movie. There were cars driving by them and Frank knew they could not see her. They weren't tuned in and she was his girl.

"How did you die, Josette, if you don't mind me asking?" he said.

"I just got very sick and fell down into the grave. I was falling for about a month before the casket caught me," she said.

"Did the werewolf not kill me because I was chosen?"

"That is correct. You are meant for bigger and better things. Werewolves are a force of darkness. They are on the same side as us."

"What's the deal with all these werewolves around all of a sudden?"

"I don't have all the answers, Frank, but the world is very unstable right now. Things are coming to a head, and that is causing things to come out of the woodwork that normally would be hidden."

"Things like werewolves?"

"Yes, Frank, things like werewolves and other things too probably."

"Spooky. Will you be with me always, Josette?"

"When you want me, I will be, but I can go other places, even small places. I could hide in your ring," Josette said.

He was wearing a pentagram ring encrusted with an emerald in the center pentagon of the pentagram. To prove this point she turned into a sort of smoke and flew into the emerald. She was gone and Frank thought maybe he had hallucinated the entire episode for a moment before she came back.

"I like it in there. It's green and warm. The grave is cold—as you will know sometime soon."

"That's very reassuring, Josette. So what do you think I should do now?"

"I don't know. Frank. What do you think you should do?" she said back in her little ethereal singsong voice.

"Oh, I know what I have to do. Josette. I've been missing some time recently and it all comes back to this other graveyard. I think if I go back there I'll find some answers."

"Let's go my cemetery man."

With that she smiled at him and it gave him the chills, but he smiled back.

Chapter 7
The Sand Hillside Strangler Strikes Again

It had been a busy month for the Sand Hillside Strangler, and he paced back and forth in his garage. He was letting himself feel angry. There was another killer out in Augusta, and the murders were all being attributed to the Sand Hillside Strangler. He did not like this. He did not want people worshiping false idols. Too many cooks in the kitchen. That's not the way it worked. He wanted it to be clear. He was determined to find the interloper.

A normal killer would be happy about this, after all he was getting more glory and it must be messing up the investigation. He didn't worry about the cops though, he didn't worry at all. He was feeling groovy. Don't worry be happy, I'll find you soon enough.

He had traveled the world in his youth with the military and studied with spiritual masters of every discipline. He had climbed many mountains. His techniques and knowledge of the underlying linking truths was unsurpassed. He lit some jasmine incense and sat on the floor in the lotus position behind his 1965 Cadillac Deville.

He was a master of the temple and within a minute he was able to achieve astral projection. He floated up out of his body. He waved his astral arm in front of his face. It was a translucent blue.

He floated up out of the garage and into the night sky.

He was floating down Western Ave looking for signs of extreme emotion or violence. When he kept focused he saw any extreme emotions as a sort of reddish vapor in the air. He saw a few tendrils coming out of a house. He floated down and entered through the wall. Just domestic violence though. He kept on searching, but it seemed that the city was safe for the night.

He opened his eyes. He had hoped he'd be able to tune into the imposter and catch him in the act but no luck yet.

I need to find out when he will strike next so I know when to look. Enough of this malarkey, he thought and walked back into the house.

"How's it going, dear?" his pretty wife asked.

"I think I've had my fill of tinkering on that old girl for today. I think I'll go out for a while."

"All right honey, should I still cook my special tuna surprise?"

"Oh yes, I'll be back in time for dinner. I'm just going to work on my game a little."

"You men and your bowling. You're all the same. See you at six then."

He kissed her on the cheek goodbye and grabbed his bowling ball bag. He tossed it in his red Ford truck and drove off.

He was planning on going to kill someone and had only been using bowling as an excuse to go out, but on second thought he decided he would go bowl a string and loosen up a little. Try and get his mind in order.

The bowling alley was a center of calm in a disorganized universe. The smooth sound of the balls rolling down the lanes. The silly music that had been current ages ago rumbling away and the machines that would give you soda, candy bars, and other small snacks.

It was a reliable place where you could even get yourself a semi-cold beer or over-priced tiny pizza and mix with the young, the old and the crippled. He went and bought a soda and asked for lane 11 as it was free. It was his lucky lane.

He bowled a 227. It did not make him happy or sad. It wasn't about the game to him. It was another form of meditating and purifying his mind. It was about the numbers. He was focusing his energy. His body went through the motions of playing the game while he sharpened the knife he had created from his mind. He had been feeling a little tapped from his astral travels.

He could have thrown a perfect game if that was his goal, for his mind was very powerful and he could do many things with it that others could not. 227 was what he wanted today and 227 was what he rolled. The clockwork order of the world brought a smile to his face that would precede the coming chaos.

He played on a league sometimes and he played as one of the better players but not as the best. He had learned a lot about people from playing on the league.

The bowling made him feel better but now it was time for murder. It was a check list in his head. Bowl a string, check. Murder a stranger, better work on getting that one checked off, because I do want to make it home in time for wifey's delicious tuna casserole. He put his street shoes back on and got back to his truck.

He drove around in a manner that any observer would have said was random, but that would not be quite accurate. He was letting his instincts be his guide, and when the turns felt right he took them. The times it did not pay off were very few and this was not one of those times.

There she was, up on the right side of the road.

Hitchhiking of all things, didn't these girls ever learn? The urge to be raped and murdered was just too hard to suppress in some. He pulled over and waited. He felt like he was at one of those fifties burger joints where the waitress brought your food to your car on roller skates.

He reached across the seat and opened the door. A cold and disheveled blonde got in. Her lip was pierced in the middle. She looked in her early twenties he eyeballed. She was pretty but in a rough sort of way. She had a slight look of wear older than her years about her that a lot of the young girls had these days.

"Thanks for picking me up, mister, it's getting pretty cold out," she said, shivering in her jeans and sweatshirt in the cab of a monster's truck.

"No problem. It wouldn't be gentlemanly to pass by a damsel in distress. Where ya headed?"

"I'm going to my boyfriend's house. He lives down at the end of Hospital Street. You heading that way?" She smiled like a puppy begging for bacon.

"Ayuh, I'm on my way to East Pittston so I'm going right by there. I don't mind dropping you there."

"Thanks a lot hon, you're a real life saver." She paused and reached over and squeezed his thigh for a second before continuing.

"Do you mind I smoke?"

"Sure, go ahead."

"Want one?"

He was surprised to find that he did.

"Well, I don't normally, but what the heck, why not? You have to live a little sometimes, don't you?"

"That's right, sugar, I like your attitude." She put two Camel lights in her mouth and lit them with a small orange plastic lighter. She passed him one. He rubbed the end of the filter against his shirt before placing it to his lips.

"I have to go see my man Lee, but I'm afraid he's gonna be mad at me."

"And why would anyone be mad at someone as pretty as you?" She did a good job at pretending to blush.

"Well, you see, I really needed fifty bucks to buy my mother's cancer medicine. The insurance covers most of the costs but the co-pays are still a real bitch, ya know. Well anyway, so Lee didn't have the money to spare all he had was the rent money. I talked him into giving me the fifty from his rent money because my sister was supposed to meet me later at Mom's and give me the fifty dollars back and a ride. She never showed up so now I'm screwed, and my man won't even be able to pay the rent. He is gonna be so mad."

She was a good actress, he gave her that. A normal person would probably buy it but he could tell it was only a pitch. Who the hell had he picked up? He smiled.

"Is that a fact? Why that is terrible. I am very sorry to hear that."

"I'm afraid it's even worse than that, for you see Lee is a violent man, and I'm scared he's gonna beat me for losing the rent money. I know you probably think I'm crazy or stupid or both for going to him when I know what's going to happen but it would only be worse if I didn't go right there and I do love him. So you can see I'm really desperate to get him his fifty bucks."

"Yeah, I wish there was something I could do to help."

"Oh, do you? Do you really? If you could find it in your heart to let me borrow the fifty dollars I'd be seriously in your debt."

"I'd like to help, but that's kind of a lot of money to be loaning a stranger, even one as pretty as you."

This game was getting fun.

"I know it is, but I'm really desperate, so desperate I'd probably do something I would never normally do if you loaned me the money. Something you might like even."

"How do you know what I like?"

"I'm full grown, I know what a man likes. What a man needs. I see that ring on your finger and I can tell you got needs your wife probably doesn't fulfill, and if you'd loan me the money, why, I couldn't help but want to suck your dick, mister. You'd like that wouldn't you, having me suck your pee pee right here in this truck? No one would ever have to know about it. It'd be our little secret."

"A tempting offer, but it takes more than that for a man like me."

"Well if you wanted to loan me a little more maybe we'd work something out. I'm flexible baby."

"First I have an important question for you and I need an honest answer."

"Don't worry, I'm clean, I've been tested. I wouldn't shit you."

"That's not what I was going to ask. I want to know if you know the Sand Hillside Strangler?"

"The Strangler, no, of course I don't know him." She grew quiet for the first time since getting into his truck, and her street smarts kicked in.

"You're scaring me. I think I want to get out now," she said quietly.

His fist moved fast and connected with her face, causing a small amount of blood to spray against the window. She tried to open the door but it wouldn't budge.

"Are you lying to me? Do you know him?"

"No! I swear I don't know him. Please just let me go. I won't say anything. I just want to go. Please, please!" She started to cry and blood and snot ran down her face.

"No, play time is over and it's time to face the facts. You met the Sand Hill Side Strangler when you got in this truck. The real strangler. There's a pretender to the throne out there, and he will pay. All challengers to the throne will be annihilated. Additionally, I'm not gonna let you go, I'm going to kill you. I don't have long to savor these petty human emotions and I intend to make the most of them."

"No, please you don't have to I'll do anything. Anything at all," she shrieked.

"Death is the most important part of life. I'm really doing you a favor."

"Oh yeah, why don't you kill yourself then, if death is so important, you asshole!"

"It's not my time, it's your time. I need this experience. Energy is eternal. Death is an illusion. Don't take it so personal."

She threw her body at him and tried to attack, but he glanced at her and she was immobilized.

"I have drugged you via a needle in the seat, if you are wondering why you cannot move," he ad-libbed.

Sometimes it was fun to say outrageous things. The truth was even more outrageous: he was holding her still because it was his will. She wasn't ready for that kind of conversation, but maybe she would be some day.

"Being afraid of death is like being afraid of an ice cube melting. It's not gone, it just became water. I'm just gonna melt your ice cube sweetheart, and it is way better to be water than ice. Solid is such a confining state. You'll be much freer this way. Would you rather be a disease-ridden whore, or fly around through the cosmos exploring eternity on the wings of forever? I think that you'll decide I'm right . . . later . . . after you're dead. Yes, I can sense your sickness that you would have shared so willingly with me. Naughty, naughty! You have no secrets from me, for I am your mother and your father reversed. I am the head of the snake and you are the tail I will eat."

He was no longer letting her speak. He knew what she would say, they all said the same few things. That part got a little monotonous. He would skip it this time. He formed hands around her throat with his mind and strangled her. He kept her on the brink a few times and choked her out. He did not kill her yet. He just let her body crumple down onto the floor of the truck's cab.

He did enjoy killing people. He also enjoyed torturing people. He was able to feed off of their suffering and pain. It made his powers stronger and stronger. He did not always torture them. He liked variety in the game. Sometimes he would make love with his victims, both alive and dead, but this time he would not. He had dinner at six.

He drove out into the woods where they could be alone and where he could stretch his legs. He got to his spot in about twenty minutes. He reached behind the seat and grabbed the rope to make the noose. He was able to get it up over the branch of his secluded old hanging tree before she started to stir.

Her eyes screamed but that was all she could manage as he removed her from the truck and stood her by the tree.

He took a box cutter out of his pocket and slit her sweatshirt and the shirt underneath from the neck down and removed them so she stood topless in the cold. He left her jeans on her, and carved the arcane symbols of power into her flesh. He sliced five symbols down in straight line from between her breasts to her belly button. He turned her around and carved the number 93 into her back.

She was ready for hanging now. Tears were running down her cheeks from the pain and the fear but she was still paralyzed. She prayed in her mind to a god she had only just begun to hope might exist that she would be saved, but she knew in her heart that she would die. He hoisted her up and watched her wiggle. It was a beautiful sunset and he felt gorged and happy inside. He got back into his truck to head back into town for his other highlight for the day, tuna surprise. He was pleased to know that the surprise was pepperoni. He'd come back later in the night for the ritual.

Chapter 8
Full Moon Over Augusta: a few days prior

Josh awoke nervous and excited on the fateful day. He had cut class. It was the first full moon since he had fucked the wolf and he knew big things would happen. He could smell the electricity in the air.

He couldn't refrain from telling Tess and she had skipped school too. That was nothing new for her. She was the most truant girl in her class.

"Brother, will you dye your hair green for me?" Tess said.

"No. I don't need to dye my hair anymore. I'm a fucking werewolf," Josh said, flexing his muscles. "I'm cool enough."

"Well, that remains to be seen doesn't it, Joshy. Come on, green hair is so hot. All guys should have green hair. Do you really think you're gonna turn into a werewolf when the moon is full? A green werewolf would be so hot."

"I don't just think it, Tess, I know it. You are going to have to leave the house. It won't be safe here for you tonight. Who knows if I'll even be aware of what's going on. If it's anything like the flicks, then I'll just be some kind of crazy animal all night and wake up naked in the park or something. That seems a little far-fetched to me, but you can't really trust anything a man in my condition might say," he said.

"And what condition is that, brother?"

"My condition is lycanthropy."

"Lying can of pee?" Tess said, and giggled.

"No, not lying can of pee. Stop being ridiculous. I said lycanthropy. It's just a fancy name for the sickness that causes werewolves. Who would have thought it was a STD, huh?" Josh said.

"That's gross. Let's smoke pot and watch cartoons now please," she said in a high pitched creepy voice. "Bunny, bunny."

"Bunny bunny, no no," he said.

"Funny bunny," she said again in the high pitched voice.

"All right, Tess, let's do it. I'll go and smoke with you and watch cartoons. But no more bunny."

They left his room for the living room. Their parents were both at work and wouldn't be home for another 5 hours so they had plenty of time to kill. Their father worked loading trucks in a warehouse and their mother was a waitress. She was still pretty so she did well with the tips.

"I don't know what's gonna happen and I gotta find out before I rip you apart or something, That's why you gotta make yourself scarce. Go over to Mama's or something. I told her to do whatever you said, you should be able to have a good time," he said.

"Why would Mama listen to you just because you fucked her?" she asked.

"When a werewolf talks, women listen," Josh said.

"Then why doesn't it work on me?" Tess said.

"'Cause you ain't no woman yet, you're still a girl," he said.

"I'm like a girl and a half at least. What about Mom and Dad?" she said.

"Who gives a shit about them?"

"Well, I don't, brother."

"So if they get eaten by me it's no big loss, right?"

"It's a big loss if I don't get to watch."

"I can understand that. Why don't we set up some secret cameras and then we can tape the whole thing. That's a good idea anyway, because then if I do black out when I wolf out, we'll have some sort of record of what I did and what I was like."

"You seem smarter than you used to be."

"Don't I, though. Who knows, I probably am. Wolves are smart animals. They need to do all kinds of smart shit like burying their weapons for the winter or whatever when they hibernate and shit."

They only had two cameras, but it was a small apartment so they were able to cover the kitchen and the living room, which were connected. That meant anything that did not happen in the bathroom or the bedrooms they would be able to catch.

Josh sent Tess away and began the waiting game. It was hellish to wait for something like this—worse even than waiting for acid to kick in, and he was starting to think nothing would happen. The parents arrived home, Mom first.

She asked where Tess was and Josh told her she was staying over at a friend's house snorting K. That was enough for her and Dad didn't even ask where she was or even notice.

Josh made himself a peanut butter sandwich and went to his room. He tried to avoid spending time with his parents whenever he could. They were very annoying and he had screaming matches with them often.

He pushed play on his CD player. He had left it on pause. The stereo kicked on without skipping a beat and Josh tried to relax to Danzig crooning about being a killer wolf.

Danzig, there's someone that might understand what I'm going through, he thought and then wondered if there was some way he could get a hold of him. Maybe I'll go track him down when I wolf out. That guy loves wolves. He'll want to talk to me for sure. Hell, he's probably a werewolf too. What if I already killed him with my slingshot?

Josh smiled. The world was starting to look like a pretty whore spreading her legs. *Camping is awesome,* he thought and was for the first time grateful he lived and loved in the great state of Maine.

He logged onto the net to check what time the Moon would rise. He wondered how the Moon was able to pay for the web site, but then he figured it was probably from all the movie cameos.

It rose at 7:16 according to the chart he found on the Moon's official site. He took off all his clothes. No use ruining good gear just in case. He waited and waited and then it happened.

It started with a sound like a howl. The sound did not escape his lips, but he heard it screaming in his brain like a thousand trains rattling the tracks. The call of the wild was a loud, piercing, never-ending wail that rattled through his being like a nitrous hit.

It was a primal hunger and it was more than in his brain, it was in his bones and it was spreading. His body was jerking and shaking. His insides felt more fluid than normal. There was intense pain at first in his spine, but that was only where it started. It spread from there and he was overcome with it. It was all he was aware of and it became him. It blinded him and he lost consciousness.

The wolf opened its eyes. He looked over at the clock and saw only a couple of minutes had gone by. *It isn't like being in the movies,* he thought, *I am in control of myself.* He could tell he was different, though. He did not like being in this small room, he did not like it at all. He wanted to run in cool night air.

He opened his second floor bedroom window and leapt out of it. He hit the ground running. It felt divine to push his new strong body, and he ran faster and faster. His nose was flooding him with information. He felt more alive than he ever had before. He headed toward Hallowell. He wanted to run in Von's Woods. He always liked it there and he was hungry. He wanted to hunt and eat something.

He ran down Sewell St. which lead him straight there. He ran fast and avoided the lights. His agility allowed him to move so he was able to avoid being seen by any people, not that there were many out in the bleak night. Those that were out he could smell and avoid long before they could detect him.

Von's woods was a public park also known as Hobbitland. There were trails through it and stone bridges over the brooks. You weren't supposed to be there at night, so of course that was when everyone liked to go. Though Josh didn't think there would be many people he'd be worrying about bothering him anytime soon.

He didn't see any cars parked by the woods so he figured it would just be him and the other animals, but he was wrong. He knew this right when he set foot in the woods. There was a lot of different smells in the woods but he was able to detect that there were two men there. He snuck up on them, practicing his stalking. They were agitated about something and the wolf could smell fresh blood on them.

He went closer to get a better look and decided to let them see him. He could tell when they did, because of the fear and urine smells. The sweet aroma of the fear intoxicated Josh. One of them said something to him, but he didn't understand it.

One of the men picked up a large stick and hit him across the chest. He hadn't expected that. He was sure he could have dodged it if his guard was up but it was the last thing he had expected from these confused looking men. They looked in their twenties and were wearing dark clothes.

Animal berserker rage crushed his restraint. He was a wolf now and ruled by the laws of the jungle. He cast aside the laws of man. He always hated them anyway for their stupidity. The wolf had been challenged. It had been attacked, and its dominance impugned by a mere mortal man. Big mistake.

The man before him was short, probably five foot four. He was about the same height Josh was in person form. The human's arms were covered with scars. Josh was thinking fast and he would act even faster.

He grabbed the one that whacked him by the shoulders and picked him up to bring his throat into his large hungry waiting wolf jaws.

Josh bit down hard and the hot delicious blood sprayed down his throat. He clenched down as hard as he could and before he realized what had happened his mouth snapped shut. He had bitten the head clean off and it tumbled on down the trail.

The other guy was standing there watching him with a stupid expression on his face. He must be catatonic with fear Josh thought as he lifted the lifeless torso and poured more hot blood down his throat like it was lemonade from a glass instead of gore from a throat hole.

He looked at the other one for a second, but then took off. He went to the other side of the woods and was surprised to notice that the one he had left alive did not flee and was talking to himself. It was weird behavior, shock Josh guessed.

Von's had provided him with as much satisfaction as it was going to he decided, so he left. He crept on down the big hill that loomed over downtown Hallowell and made his way to the Kennebec River. This was the river that divided Augusta in half. The western half was the half with Sand Hill on it. That was the side the wolf was on. He followed the river to his right which led through Farmingdale to Gardiner. If he had gone left and followed the train track he would have headed out of Hallowell and back into Augusta right at the old cemetery.

He was a fast mover and he soon arrived at the Gardiner Bridge. He dove into the river and swam across letting the water wash him clean. It was cold and invigorating.

He was starting to feel quite strange. He felt much joy. Everything was weird and funny. He started noticing things weren't quite the right shape. All the lights were looking way too bright, he had noticed that right away when he turned into a wolf, but now they were even more bright. He didn't let it throw him though, it was a familiar feeling somehow. I must be high on blood at the end of the world. Must have been something I ate. He laughed.

He continued on running faster and faster until he caught a whiff of carnage. Running was starting to feel weird. It was like he was floating along. His legs were moving but he couldn't feel them, he just had an impression of them. He could smell death and organs. He zeroed in on it, and found a girl hanging from a tree.

What was left of a girl. She was hung by her neck, and also from her bound together feet. She was facing forward and her midsection was mutilated in an extreme manner. Her feet were up behind her, putting her body into a U shape.

She had a deep vertical slice from her pubic bone to her breast bone. There was a deeper mutilation that ran horizontally across her stomach almost severing her in half making her hanging in such a drastic angle possible. Josh walked up knowing he was alone, but just barely because the scent of death was clogging his nostrils. He had never seen anything like this in real life and it was intoxicating.

"Cool," he said, though it sounded more like a growl. He went closer to investigate. She was naked except for a pair of dirty white socks on her feet. He could tell her guts and most of her organs had been removed. The lungs were left, but that seemed to be about all.

Her pubic patch looked putrid. He also saw there was a circle burned into the ground like someone had a campfire there. He put his hand down on it and it was still warm.

He felt his paw continue though the ground and bounce back up at him. The smell was making him hungry. Well, if someone had gone to all this trouble to truss up this bird and even clean it, it would be a shame for it to go to waste. *Maybe I'll have just have myself a little taste.*

He bit off a piece of flesh that was dangling from the side of the chest. He had to bite down and pull hard to rip it off, but it gave. It was delicious—much more delicious than he ever could have imagined. He chewed and chewed and tried to think of what it tasted like, but there was just not anything he could think of that came even remotely close to describing the sheer tender ecstasy of the flesh. *Yeah, I'm gonna eat some more of that.* He took a big bite out of her bulging breast.

It was excellent. *I'm glad she didn't have fake ones* he suddenly thought, then mentally added *one boob, two boob, red boob, blue boob.* Josh realized he was having a psychedelic experience at that moment.

It must be from the blood, he thought. *Wow, human blood makes you trip, that's amazing.* No wonder everyone wants to drink it. Vampires must be the biggest acid heads in the world. He kept having similar strange thoughts as he munched away at the body, devouring flesh and organ and meat alike with equal vigor and animalistic enthusiasm. He even cracked the bones in his strong teeth and sucked out the rich marrow.

This is weird but delectable. People are really tasty, *If I had known how good folks tasted I would have eaten myself a long time ago.* Everything was gone and he was fully satisfied. He howled at that old harvest moon and began walking home. There was a Black Sabbath song stuck in his head.

Chapter 9
What's the Hold Up?

"Well, lap my bag, Waldo, do you think its Halloween or something? Is this like Halloween two?" the fat redneck said, wiggling his flipper-like hand at the other girl.

"Shut your fucking asshole FACE, this is a ROB-ER-REEEEEE! Put your face against the cooler or I will show you just how fucking real this is!" Trish screamed at him. He was too wasted for much of a reaction.

"Good lord, what a mouth on you. Your daddy should wash your mouth out with soap. A robbery, you say. Why, that would mean there would have to be some robbers here. It looks more like an eighth grade costume party than a real live hold 'em up to me. Why don't you girls go on home and concentrate on your home economics or something." He was slurring a little and thought everything he said was super funny.

"I won't say this again, you fat bastard. Put your face on the cooler and shut that gaping cunt mouth," Trish shrieked. This guy was really working her last frazzled coke nerve.

"Do what she says or I'll shoot your fucking dick off!" Mildred screamed from the back.

"Well, I think if your Daddy's not gonna do it, maybe I'll wash out your mouth out with soap," the mountain man said, and advanced toward

Trish and started to close the ten foot gap between them.

Both girls pulled the trigger at the same time and the drunk was struck in the chest and side by the bullets. He slammed against a stand up M & M display and fell on the ground, bleeding to death in a pile of chocolate.

He was no longer running his mouth. One of the bullets had hit a lung and he was having a hard enough time drawing breaths, let alone to think about talking shit.

"You wanna fuck with me, asshole? Think I'm just a prissy little girl? Well how about now you fat piece of shit?" Trish whispered.

Illustrating her point further, she shot him between the legs. He bolted upright and let out a blood curdling high pitched gurgling sort of scream. Blood was coming out of his mouth and pooling out around his body.

Trish reached over and grabbed a bottle of dish soap off the shelf. She opened it and squirted the soap into the man's screaming mouth.

"Who's a little girl now, big man?" Trish continued to taunt him.

"Hey, you stole my idea, bitch!" Mildred said, walking up the aisle and ventilating the fat screaming head with her pistol.

"Yeah, well it was a good one," Trish replied.

"Should have let him suffer more. I fucking hate rednecks. What should we do about the other one?" Mildred asked.

"I don't know. What should we do about you, sir?" Trish said.

The clerk was looking pale. He had placed all the money in the bag and set it on the counter.

"Well, you don't have to worry about me, I hated that bastard. Always complaining the coffee was too old. Fuck you, man, it's fifty cents, deal with it, you know. As far as I'm concerned it was a couple of fuckin' lobstermen."

"What about the camera?" Trish asked.

"That piece of shit hasn't worked in years. Look close. It doesn't even have a tape in it."

"Well, that sounds good enough for me," Trish said, and took the money bag. She reached in and pulled out a fifty and put it on the counter.

"Here, hide this in your sock or whatever and buy yourself a quarter bag or something," she said.

"Thank you very much, but I don't think I could rightly take that."

"Suit yourself," she said and took the bill back. The girls walked out.

"You girls take care of yourselves, okay!" he called after them.

They ran out and jumped in the car, which they were glad to see was still there and running, even though they had left it unattended.

Trish tried not to drive too crazy, but the tires squealed when they left. They burst out of there fast and were back on the highway. The exit was only about a half mile from the store.

"Holy shit on a shingle, that was a rush," Mildred said, breaking the silence.

"Yeah, that was crazy. Son of a bitch shouldn't have came at me, but he did, so fuck him, he got what he deserved," Trish said.

"What do you think your Dad's gonna think?" Mildred said.

"As long as we get away clean it won't be a big deal. Don't worry I'll handle him," Trish said.

They had got on the highway going north which was away from where they wanted to go. They drove a few exits before deciding it was safe and got off the highway.

They pulled to the side of the road for a quick stop to blow the rest of the coke off the small mirror Trish had in her purse. They also took this time to stash the big bulky black sweatshirts, the guns, and the money bag in the wheel well of the car where the spare donut tire had been. They had removed it before the last robbery and it was still in Trish's garage leaning against the wall.

They were totally gakked by the time they got back on 95 south and headed back toward Augusta. They cranked up the tunes and flew down the highway at 85 mph. Mildred wondered if that was the smart thing to do but she keep it to herself. She was feeling pretty brave anyway, it seemed like a good clean get away.

"Holy shit that Tommy can play fucking fast," Mildred said.

"Yeah, my friend John once said he had seen them play live and it was the fastest guitar playing he had ever seen, and that he played it all with one hand as he swung back and forth on a rafter," Trish replied.

"That's fucking insane," Mildred said.

"I know. The Accused are badass," Trish said.

"We just killed a guy. How does that make you feel?" Millie asked.

"Wet," Trish said. "My panties are barely holding back the flood. I can feel it running down my leg a little."

"Everything makes you horny, Trish."

"Just murder and mayhem, dollface. Besides, it's not like that guy was a real person or anything. He was just a worthless fleshy shit-bag, and did you notice that gaudy gold cross around his neck? UM . . . tacky! If anything, we did the world a big favor by flushing that hunk of shit down the cosmic crapper, Mildred."

"Don't forget to wipe."

Then they heard the siren.

"Holy fucking shit, no fucking way. Goddamn it I knew we should have stashed a gun up front," Trish said.

"Don't worry or be crazy. It's just for speeding for fucks sake. They don't know anything. Just pull over and smile at the piggy. I bet we don't even get a ticket," Mildred said.

"I hope your right, Millie, and I hope that clerk stuck to his story or I swear to Satan I will hunt him down and kill him in a most painful manner," Trish hissed like she was Queen of the snakes.

She pulled the car over and hoped for a feverish minute that the cop would fly by them chasing someone else down the highway. That didn't happen this time and the state police cruiser pulled up behind them and lit up the car with its headlights.

"Just remember to be cool, Mildred, we're okay," Trish said.

"That's what I been telling you."

It seemed like forever while they waited for the cop to come.

"Oh shit, how does my nose look, can you see any coke?" Trish asked. Mildred could see a little and passed Trish a tissue in record speed.

"How do I look?" she asked.

"I can't see anything, but give it a good blow just to be safe."

A light shined in as the cop scanned the back seat and floor. That didn't last long, the car was clean and he walked around to the driver's side door. Trish rolled down her window.

"License, registration and proof of insurance, please. I'll also take your identification little miss," the Statie said.

He was right pissed off to be standing on the side of the highway on this cold night. Mildred handed over her state id card. Trish handed her license over then reached over and opened the glove box. A bunch of tampons fell out.

"Oh my god, I'm so embarrassed! I'm sorry just a minute." Both girls shrieked with laughter.

Trish fished the registration and proof of insurance from the glove box and handed it to the officer.

"Do you know why I pulled you over this evening?" he said.

"I'm like so sorry, I know I was speeding it was bad," Trish confessed.

"It's dangerous to drive that fast. The speed limits are there to protect you girls. Why were you in such a hurry?" the policeman asked.

"I'm really sorry. It just like, Millie's Dad will ground her if she's not home on time and we're supposed to go to the Devastator Maximus concert at the civic center this Saturday and now we're not gonna be able to go, and I'm having my period, and everything is terrible and I know it's all my fault." With that flagrant admission Trish started crying. The officer sighed and slowly backed away.

"Calm down Miss. You two sit tight here for a minute and I'll be right back." The state policeman walked back to his cruiser.

"Do you think he bought it?"

"Yeah, I think so," Trish said, while continuing to cry.

"The tampons in the glove box was brilliant."

"You like that? Yeah, I always keep some there. I can't take credit for it though, I read it in Ladies Bone Journal," Trish said.

"Ha ha I'll have to remember that when I get a car. Like we'd go see Devastator Maximus, I almost lost it when you said that," Millie said.

"I know, they are like soooo gay. Motherfucker, I just want this to be over with. It's taking forever. If we make it back home I'm gonna roll us the biggest fucking blunt, you won't be able to tell if you're smoking it or earning an A," Trish said.

The horrible waiting was over and the cop came back.

"Excuse me, Miss Ackerman, I'm going to be letting you off this time. You are lucky I pulled you over, because I'm only letting you go because I know your father and I know you're good girls. Criminal speeding for a minor would result in you losing your license, so slow it down and drive safe."

They thanked him and he went back to the police car and turned on his lights so that they were able to get back into the flow of traffic.

"Wow, lucky fucking break, huh?" Mildred said.

"I guess," Trish said thoughtfully.

"We should try and call Frank when we get back. We don't want anything to go wrong," Mildred said.

"You're right, as usual," Trish said.

They continued home without event. Trish gave Millie some watermelon flavored blunt wraps and counted the money.

"How did we do?" Millie asked.

"Two hundred and thirty seven dollars," Trish said.

"So that's how much a redneck's life costs?" Millie said.

"No, that was free of charge. 237's just my hourly rate."

Chapter 10
Back to the Start

Frank walked back in the front door of his house. Nayte and Dan sat in the living room playing a game of cribbage.

"Fifteen fucking two you limber dicked fucker!" Nayte cried, advancing his red peg when Frank opened the door. Frank picked up the bong and took a welcome home hit. Josette flew out of his ring and Frank stumbled back shocked. She flew right through his friends and began floating in slow circles near the ceiling. Frank gasped and fell backward onto the floor.

"That must have been a good one," Dan said, pausing to look up at Frank before continuing with his move. Frank waited for them to notice or say something about Josette but they didn't.

"Sorry, I just wanted to take a look around," Josette called from above Frank's head, giggling.

"Oh, it's cool, I just need to get used to this."

"What's that?" Nayte asked.

"We're not gonna talk about that."

"Okay . . . where did you go?"

"I walked down to the graveyard by Bolley's Famous Franks."

"Holy shit, you went all the way there and back? That's far, must be a couple of miles away. You were trucking."

"I guess I must have been motorvated. Hey, speaking of motorvating, Nayte, do you mind if I borrow your ride for a little bit?"

"Borrow my van, why?"

"There's somewhere I need to go. Another graveyard I was in a few days ago. I think I left something there and I need to get it."

"What did you leave there?"

"Answers, Nayte, just answers. Graveyard business, you know."

"Do you want us to go with you?" Dan offered.

"No, I think I can handle it myself. I just gotta move quickly if you know what I mean."

"Oh, time sensitive, I dig," Dan said.

"You guys stay here and finish the cribbage tournament and I'll be back in a little bit and we'll smoke up the rest of that bag. Sound cool?"

"That's cool with me. I left the keys in it. You gotta get your own car, though. My god, man, you're old."

"All right. I'll work on it."

They were interrupted by the phone ringing. They let the answering machine pick it up as was the household custom to dodge bill collectors. The greeting was Frank strumming an acoustic guitar for a minute and yelling "leave a message." It was very punk.

"Hello . . . hello . . . Charlie, this is . . . your sexy Sadie." That was followed with giggling and Frank could make out Trish saying "you're so gay" in the background. Frank picked up the phone.

"Frank's Morgue, you stab 'em we slab 'em."
More laughter.

"Hey, sexy, whatcha doing tonight?" Mildred said.

"Hey, Millie, uh, I was just on my way out to return some video tapes."

"Oh yeah, Bateman, sounds like a barrel of strippers. Wanna come out and play with us instead?"

"I'd really like to, but I'd hate to get late fees."

"You men are all alike. No staying power. First you quote American Psycho and now you won't even sport-fuck me."

"Aw, doll, come on, don't worry about it. I'll see you soon. I just can't right now. I got some things to take care of tonight, but how about we get together like tomorrow night?"

"I hate waiting, but you're worth it. We don't like people usually ever, Frank. We really like you. That means something. We are the same kind of people as you, and we are so glad to have found you. If you need anything, make sure you know you can count on us, all kidding aside, you got it?"

"I know I can. It seems crazy, but I know it. Thanks for calling. I haven't been able to think about much else since I met you. I even dreamed about you two last night. Don't worry, I'll be safe, and I'll see you soon."

"You better, mister. Well, I am horny, and if you don't have the time to help out, I'm just gonna have to go and hump Trish's face some more."

"Hot. Take a picture for me. Sounds like a real Kodak moment."

"We'll see."

"Goodbye, Millie."

"Goodbye, Frank." Frank hung up the phone.

"Someone's gonna get some pus-say!" Nayte called out and lewdly shook his hips. Frank couldn't help but smile.

"What can I say, I'm lover not a spider."

Dan smiled at that one.

"Well, gents, in the immortal words of my father, it's been real, it's been fun, but it ain't been real fucking fun. I'll catch you cool cats later." Frank was out the door, cutting the deck before he left as always. This time he got the Devil card, major arcana number 15. It was a good sign and he walked out happy.

Nayte drove a big old blue Chevy Van, which he used to haul around musical equipment. It was an old girl but there was still some life in her yet. It was the kind of van you wouldn't want to drive by a school in. It took a couple of tries to start, but it always started. Well, almost always. It started this time.

Frank drove out Route 202 and began looking for the cemetery. He drove and drove and did not see it. After a while Frank decided he must have gone too far and turned back around. He turned on the high beams and drove half the speed limit.

He spotted the small old cemetery. Frank pulled over and parked the van.

As soon as he got out he could see the shack he had woken up in, and knew he was at the right place.

"Josette, can you hear me?" he called.

"I can always hear you, Frank."

He looked to the right and there she was. She had a bright red sparkly bow in her hair though this time.

"Hey, I like that bow. It's very fetching."

She smiled.

"Can you tell me if anyone's here in the graveyard?"

"Let me see."

She floated up in the air and took off. It did not take her long.

"No one is here now, but a little dead boy told me there was a creep here earlier and he left something here by one of the tombs."

"Excellent. I don't know how I ever got along without you, Josette. Take me there." She floated and he followed down into the depths of the graveyard. It was bigger than it looked and they went down a hill to a cluster of tombs in a grove of trees. It was very dark here but Frank was having no trouble seeing.

He saw it right away, sitting there on a grave with a rock on top of it. He picked up the rock and put it in his coat pocket. Underneath was a yellow envelope. He opened it and inside was a birthday card. It had a picture of a cartoon birthday cake on it with the caption "Happy Birthday!" Frank opened the card. It was the talking kind that you could record a 10 second message on.

"Kill him, kill him, kill him!" the card exclaimed in a very gruff hoarse voice. Inside the card was a Polaroid picture. He bent close to study it and it was the man who had been after Disco—Jack Valenti. The picture was bent like it had been in someone's pocket.

This case is getting more and more peculiar, he thought as he looked at the picture. He played the card's message over and over again but could not recognize the voice, though it sounded familiar. He stood there pondering what this meant, listening to the songs of the dead in the darkness, but still was not able to come up with any answers.

"Eyes stare out into the darkness with no form," he sang to himself, and started walking back to the van.

"What do you think it means, Josette?" he asked.

"What do I think it means, Frank? I think it means you should kill that person right away," Josette said, floating beside him. "You are meant for murder."

"I don't know, Josette . . . I think your right. Jack Valenti must die. He's a tough guy so it's not going to be easy. How come you're so smart for an eight year old?"

"I only have the 'body' of an eight year old Frank. I have the mind of someone who's a hundred and thirty. But really, I'm even older, because I had a few other lives before this one, and so have you for that matter."

"Bullshit. I'm not sure if that's something to brag about anyway."

"Funny. You are quite a card. Are you going to go get stoned now?"

"No, I'm afraid it's not quite time for the bong hit good night. Nope. I need some more information. If I'm gonna mess with a major player like Valenti, I'm gonna need more information."

"You should be careful—you must kill him if you want to amount to anything, Frank."

"No doubt about it, someone most definitely is trying to use me, but there's no time to worry about that. Valenti is gonna be gunning after me for hitting him with that bottle anyway. I was going to try and lay low because he doesn't know me, I'm not in those kinds of heavy circles you know but I might as well just kill this guy. It's a two birds with one stone sort of deal, but I am gonna need some intel. It's time to go back to the barn."

"I'm sleepy. Mind if I take a nap?"

"No, go ahead. I'll call you if I need you."

He headed for good old Elm St and parked in the spot beside the driveway. No one was fucked up enough to be outside tonight he noticed. Frank got out and locked it. He walked along the driveway and came to the door at the end. He banged on it and waited. No one answered of course, so he tried the knob. It was locked.

He reached into his back pocket and took out his wallet. He slipped the lock with his Shaw's Supermarket Rewards Card and walked in, taking the immediate left up the stairs. He locked the door behind him. The barn was empty and he opened the door into Lia's adjoining apartment. The first door led into a entranceway where you could go into the apartment on your left or a storage room on your right. He went left walking into the kitchen.

"Hello?" he called.

"Who's that?" a curt voice shot out.

"It's just me, Frank, I need to talk to you."

"Again? Well, welcome back Frank come on into the living room." He walked forward through the kitchen turning right and walked through a beaded curtain to the living room. He noticed there was a chain with a doll's arm hanging from it, in the center of the beads.

The living room was dark. It was lit with a blue light and the walls were covered with various pictures of people they knew mixed in with rock stars, pornography, and pictures from medical textbooks. Lia sat on the dirty carpet on a large tasseled pillow. She was wearing her trusty sunglasses and smoking a black clove cigarette. He did not see anyone else in the room. She squinted at him when he walked in.

"Are you alone?" Frank asked.

"No, I was just having some fun with Linda, but I wore the poor girl out." Lia put two fingers to her lips and dropped her long tongue between them and cackled.

"No one can keep up with me," she added in a sing song falsetto voice.

"Good for you!" Frank said.

"Come on, we can go and talk in the barn. You're not alone either. I see a little girl with you."

"Yeah, she's been hanging out all night. She's cool."

"You're a shy one, ain't you," Lia said, pointing at his ring. They started to walk out when a whiny voice came out from around the corner.

"If you're gonna go out in the barn and talk can you at least get me a beer first, I'm naked," Linda called out from the adjacent bedroom through the doorless doorway.

"Yeah, yeah, don't get naggy." Lia looked at him and shrugged then added, "women," and shook her head. She ducked around the corner and grabbed a forty from the fridge and ran it into the bedroom.

Lia led the way into the barn and walked to the center of the room pulling a cord that turned on the Xmas lights. It was chilly out there, but a safe place to talk.

"So what's up?" she asked, lighting a smoke.

"Oh, just my dick, interested?"

"Sorry, but you know I only take dick on special occasions, and this don't seem all that special."

"All right, hot stuff, cool down. What I really need is to find out what you know about Jack Valenti. Where he can be found, anything like that?"

"What's this about?"

"You're better off not knowing," he said, and she sighed.

"I will trust your judgment on that one. You and me, we're close so I'll try and help you the best I can. He is a serious customer though, and if you or someone you know is gonna tangle with him they had better be careful. He is a killer, and a thief and an evil man. You're an evil man too Frank . . . but I like you better."

"You say he's a killer. Are you sure? What's the deal with that?"

"Do you remember Jeffrey Lee?"

"I used to hear the name, but I never knew him."

"He was the kind of guy that just pushes his luck as far as it will go. He didn't think enough about whose toes he stepped on. He was getting out of hand and the kind of people that never lose money were losing money, so someone gave the order and Valenti is supposed to have been the enforcer."

"Who gave the order, who's his boss?"

"Nobody seems to know for sure the answer to that question. Some people say it came from

Jimmy Cartucci, some say it was Rev Petafye, and others who were scared to even suggest elude that the order came from the mayor."

"The mayor, are you serious, you think he's dirty? I just thought he liked to deny mythical beasts and shit like that."

"I have no idea what the mayor does, but I know he is more powerful than your average mayor and he must be hiding something because I am not able to learn anything about him. He is shielded, which seems a little suspicious for a mayor."

"Well, anyway the mayor doesn't matter to me, its Valenti I'm concerned with. So what did he do to Jeffrey Lee?"

"He took him out to the West Gardiner Rod and Gun Club for target shooting and took a shotgun and blew his legs off below the knees. Lee lay on the ground screaming and Valenti said he had a message to deliver to Lee before he died, and then he pissed on him. Then he wraps old Jeffrey Lee's head in duct tape so he can't scream. He had a small metal basin with cement in it. He put Lee in it and it fit him from the knee stumps to the waist. Then he is supposed to have brought him to an ice fishing shack and just dropped him down into the river."

"Wow, a cement overcoat, that's so cool. I can't believe people still do that. That's kind of classy." It almost made him not want to kill the guy.

"Ice fishing can be some crazy shit in these parts. Always more people go then come back."

"Sacrifices to the mighty Kennebec River."

"That's the only story I know about the guy, but I'm sure there's more so be careful."

"How do you know this stuff?"

"Hey, people talk to me. I'm a witch."

"All right. Now where could this guy be found."

"He lives in Gannet Estates. He has been known to drink down at Richard's Lounge in the evenings."

"Thanks, that should be useful."

"Anything else I can do to help?"

"Would you mind reading my cards, or would that just be annoying?"

"I got the time, for you," Lia said, and went and got a well-worn deck of playing cards. She never used tarot cards, only regular cards for divination. She had told him it had been passed down to her from her grandmother. Lia was of gypsy stock. She passed the deck of cards to Frank.

"Shuffle until you feel the cards are in the right position then cut twice to the right." He did as she said.

"Are you old or are you young?" He always had to think about that one a while. Sometimes he felt young and sometimes he felt old. He felt young today, maybe eternally.

"Young."

She flipped three cards face up. It was the queen of hearts, the queen of diamonds, and the ace of spades.

"Hmmmm, let me see here. I see two women around you, important women, but only recently acquainted to you. Does that make sense to you?"

"Complete sense."

"I'm not sure if they are good witches or bad witches, but they are surrounded by danger, so that means you are in danger through your association with them." She grew silent for a minute and tilted her head back and forth, then tapped the queen of diamonds twice.

"These girls do not mean you harm, I don't think. But they are hiding something from you. I see masks on these girls. There's more here than meets the eye. You need to watch out for bad luck. Here, I got something for you." Lia pulled a necklace with an upside down ankh on it and put it around his neck.

"Wear this and it will bring you luck. Now you can ask the cards three yes or no questions if you like. You don't have to voice them aloud." She passed him the cards again and directed him to shuffle them while focusing on the question. He had to think for a minute. *Am I becoming a vampire?* She told him to flip the cards face up one by one. She stopped him after the first card. It was the queen of hearts.

"The answer is a very definite yes."

Frank paused a moment to collect his thoughts. "All right, I'm ready." *Should I kill Jack*

Valenti? Frank shuffled. He flipped over the cards and right away she told him to stop, and his answer was the king of hearts.

"It is most definitely a yes, once again."

"Well, I guess that's that. Hmm, I got one more." He shuffled for the last time and thought *Will I get in any trouble with the police if I kill him?* He flipped the cards and they went about half way through the deck before they landed on the ten of spades.

"That's a no, but it's not certain."

"Okay, thanks a lot. You've been a real life saver. I better get Nayte's van back to him. I'll see you soon."

"Okay, bring me another bottle of wine next time you come over and you will have better luck. Say hi to Nayte and Dan for me. Tell them to get off their lazy asses and come over here some time."

"I'll pass it along. Goodbye, darling."

"See you later soon," she said, and gave him a big hug. She wanted him to pick her up and spin her around and he did.

"Don't worry, Frankie, it'll all work out. You'll see." Then she cackled.

"I think it might this time. I really do, that's the funny part," Frank said, and headed home.

Chapter 11
A Morbid Beginning

The Sand Hillside Strangler couldn't stop thinking about werewolves. It was excellent they were here. Reports from reliable residents confirmed it. Of course, there was an article in the paper where the Mayor debunked the werewolf scare as a hoax, but there was always a cover-up.

He got in his trusty truck and drove out to where he had left her. There was nothing left but blood and gore on the ground. It was amazing. The end really was near. He had carved the proper symbols into her flesh, and came back later that night and disemboweled her.

He had performed the Rite of Virilis. He had read it in a book of German black magic. He had eaten the organs and left the rest for the beast. He had sat under the moon eating the unclean parts.

He was glad it was not in vain and the werewolf had come and taken his sup. Now they were connected, and it would be different the next time the wolf came out.

He had lived in Augusta his whole life and had seen a lot of strange things. Things happened here that should not happen anywhere with startling regularity. Maine was a hotspot in general because it had so much uncharted area, but Augusta had been an epicenter for weird activity for generations. Even the chupacabra was having trouble hiding here.

He knew there was a conspiracy to keep this from the general public. Too many government officials came here. He still hadn't been able to locate the copycat but he was working on it. The subjugation of the false prophet was an important step in the greater ritual. It would only be a matter of time, he always got what he wanted. It was a benefit of being superior.

He was meditating to try and figure out what he would do next. After a while he began to get very tired and he allowed himself to fall asleep. Sometimes his dreams offered him guidance or showed him the future. This time he dreamed of the past. The long ago time when he was just a boy.

He dreamed of the day he had his first encounter with death. It began innocently enough. He was eight years old, and it was in July. It was a hot day and when the ice cream truck song went off, all of the children from Sand Hill flocked to it. Even the young strangler, who had in those days been called Franklin, raced toward the truck. He stopped twenty feet away and just watched as the other children got their Rocket Pops, and Choco-Tacos. He wanted an ice cream treat like the other children, but his family was poor and he did not have any money.

A man walked by and looked at him. He smiled at young Franklin and handed him a five dollar bill. He knew he shouldn't but could not resist taking it. The man smiled a strange smile and walked away without another word. Little Franklin was just in time to get a Fudgsicle and an ice cream sandwich made out of two chocolate chip cookies.

He was eating these ice cream treats and walking along feeling very happy. He was walking down the street to visit his friend Ben, who lived just around the corner. His friend wasn't home, so Franklin started walking back. He decided to take a shortcut through a patch of woods.

He was thirty feet into the woods when he saw the man who had given him the money again. There was a difference. This time he was hanging from a tree with a belt around his neck. Franklin was frozen in place.

He stood there and stared at the body, it looked so weird. Peaceful, yet grotesque, with the leather belt cutting into the throat and the eyes bulging out.

He stayed there for what seemed like a long while just staring and then he went home. He decided not to tell anyone about this. It was his secret thing and he knew if he told that they would take it away from him.

His bedtime was eight o'clock but he pretended he was tired, and was in bed by 7:30. By eight o'clock he decided it was time. He put a bunch of stuffed animals in his bed under the covers in case his parents looked in on him, but he doubted they would. They were inattentive.

His method of escape was through the window. His bedroom was on the second story of the apartment but it had a wooden ladder against it for a fire escape. He had only used it once before. His cousin, Salazar, had locked him in his room, and he had gone out the window and escaped the prank.

He was a little frightened to go alone into the dark but he could not help himself. He wanted to see if it was real, as he had half convinced himself that he had imagined the whole thing. But he still had four dollars and twenty cents in change, so he knew at least that was real.

It didn't take him long to get to the woods again, but he hesitated before stepping inside. He must know he decided and stepped out of the dim light of the street lamp and into the ubiquitous dark of the woods.

He walked down the path and his eyes adjusted so he could see a little bit. The moon was mostly full too and that helped, though at first he wondered if he would even be able to find the body in the dark. But after only a few steps in, it turned out he didn't need to see it because he could smell it. He followed his nose and soon he was standing in front of the pine tree with the man dangling from it once again.

He gasped when he saw the man. Even though he knew what he would find it was more scary this time. In the dark the man's face was unclear and if he tried to focus his eyes on it then it began to change and become even more hideous.

He wanted to run away but he could not move a muscle. Then the horrible thing moved. Its head swung directly to face him and it stared at him with eyes that glowed a hateful red.

Franklin felt a scream well up and catch in his throat. Even screaming was beyond his current capabilities. He could see the corpse's jaw moving up and down and it was licking its lips with a disgusting swollen brown tongue.

The corpse reached one hand up to the belt around its neck and snapped it off in a single graceful movement and dropped without a sound to the ground. It landed upright and stretched its arms and neck with a terrible cracking sound. Then the horrible thing spoke.

"Have you come here to learn or to die, young one?" It stared directly at him, and it made a sort of strange sense all of a sudden, like when the final piece of a jigsaw puzzle snaps in and reveals the picture in a surprising revelation that you should have been able to see coming but were for some reason unable to until this one crystal clear moment in time that seemed to last forever and ever.

"I have come here to learn." He had finally found his voice and the words had rolled off his tongue with conviction and purpose beyond his years.

"Learning is hard, most never learn. Dying is easy, everyone dies. What makes you so special that you deserve this hidden knowledge? Answer me wrong once and I will bite out one of your eyes. Answer me wrong twice and I will bite off your puny little boy cock and spit it in your father's face."

"What makes me so special, sir? I was born to do great things, I just know it. I have always known it. Known that I was meant for more than this. I've always felt out of place around the others, they are not like us. You're not like me either, but you are better than them like me. I would learn what you would teach me." It didn't even feel like it was him speaking the words, that wasn't the way he spoke. The words just ran out of his mouth of their own volition.

The body before him undulated and writhed, one of its eyes rolling down its check before it spoke again.

"Yes, you have a talent, boy, It is true. Not much now, but someday if you live that long, who knows. You could be something special. If I want you to be. If I let you be. Would you kill for the power you seek, child?"

"Yes, I would, anyone, it wouldn't matter. People don't matter they are only toys."

"What mature philosophy you have, young one." With those words the creature flung itself forward at a preternatural speed and clenched his bony hands around Franklin's throat and began to strangle him. It completely cut the air off as it picked him up and put its face against Franklin's. It was disgusting and rotting and lukewarm. He could feel muscles and bones rubbing against his face as he started to black out. The thing licked his check in a long slow slurp and allowed him to breathe again.

"Expect the unexpected. Know that death is inevitable and always immediately attainable. I present you with a choice now. There is a trail to my right, you may walk down it and away from me, and it is most likely that we will never see each other again, or you can take the trail to my left and become my student. In doing this you acknowledge I give you three days to give me a human sacrifice. Do this and you will be rewarded with power far beyond what you know is possible. Fail me and, well, let's just say you really don't want to fail me." The horrible thing laughed a laugh that sounded like cats screwing.

"Meet me here at midnight of the day the deed is done. If you're not here on midnight of the third night I will come for you. Choose wisely young architect."

"May I ask you a question, sir?"

"You may ask me one question, and then you must choose."

"Are you the man that bought me the ice cream?"

"No, he killed himself, he is but a vessel now, as you should someday aspire to be. I am beyond the frailties of the flesh. Now go child." Franklin did not hesitate any longer. He was too terrified not to go. After all he was only an eight year old boy. He walked immediately down the left path and hurried away.

He may have only been an eight year old boy, but he knew this was too good a chance to pass up. The only thing he had to figure out was who he could kill. He only had three days to pull this off, or else.

The answer came to him at lunch the next day at school. It was Meredith. Meredith must die. She lived on his street and they sometimes played together. At lunch he asked her if she wanted to play after school. She said okay. He said he had a surprise to show her. She was excited about it.

When school was over they rode the bus home together. She was wearing a white shirt with a brown duck on it. They sat together in the middle of the yellow bus. They did not always sit together, but it wasn't uncommon.

"Come on, tell me what the surprise is, Franklin," Meredith pleaded with him.

"It's a surprise, silly. Don't you want to be surprised?"

"Yeah, but I gotta go home first, and tell my Mommy."

"We don't have time for that. We have to go now and then afterwards we can go to your mom's."

"Mommy will be mad if I don't come right home after school. I don't wanna get in trouble."

"Fine, I'll tell you the surprise then if you insist, and then you'll know why you have to go with me first."

"What's the surprise?"

"I got a pony! It's tied up in the woods now."

"Why would a pony be in the woods, Franklin?"

"He's in there because my Uncle Mike left him there. My parents wouldn't give me a pony, but my Uncle Mike did. He went to talk to them about it to try and convince them to let me bring it back home."

"Well, I just have to go home for a second and tell my Mommy first," Meredith said. Her whole face was glowing at the thought of ponies.

"We don't have time. That pony's been tied up all day and he's hungry. My uncle said I had to go to him right away after school and bring him some apples."

"He doesn't have anything to eat?"

"No, I have a bag of apples for him in my back pack, you can help me feed them to him, and then we'll go to your Mom's house and tell her. Then we'll go back and ride the pony!"

"Yay!" Meredith cheered with him. She could no longer resist the allure of the pony, it was just too amazing. She wanted to know all the details about it, and he filled her in and told her how he wanted her to be his first friend to see the pony because she was his best friend. She was very happy.

They got off the bus and he led her down the street and into the woods. They walked for a little bit down to where the river ran deep. He knew the time was right. He saw a big stone that would just barely fit in his hand.

"Meredith, I see him. I see the pony. Look, he's tied to that tree!" Franklin cried, and pointed down the riverbank. She took a couple steps forward to try to spot the pony. Franklin bent down and picked up the jagged rock.

"Surprise!" he said, and swung the rock as hard as he could into the back of her head. She fell forward unto the stones by the edge of the river. She started to get up, crying immediately, not understanding what was happening.

He saw there was blood running out of the back of her head, matting in her hair, spilling over her barrettes. He swung the rock again, aiming for the same spot and she was knocked forward again onto her face. She was trying to scream, but mostly choking and gasping on blood now.

She tried again to get up, but only made it to her knees before he hit her again. He noticed that she had blood all over her white Keds. When she fell down a third time, she was almost in the river. He grabbed her long, bloody blonde hair and pulled her face to the water and pushed it under. He held her face down under the water. The water was only a few inches and she struggled, but only for about a minute, then she lay still. Franklin was out of breath and scared.

He stood up and picked up his killing rock. It was covered with blood. He put it inside a paper bag in his back pack. She had not moved and her face was still under the water, so he knew she was dead. He threw her book bag into the river and pushed her body in. He got very wet, but it washed the blood off his hands.

He had her totally in the water, but she wasn't going anywhere, just stuck on the edge. He looked around until he found a long stick. He prodded her body until it was deep enough to get caught in the current. He took his bag and left.

He went to the place in the woods where the man had hung himself. There was no one there, and no sign of what had been there, but Franklin knew it was the right place. He could feel it. This place felt more intense than it had before. He could feel the power radiating. Just like he could feel the evil he was carrying in his backpack. He opened it up and removed his killing rock from the paper bag that had earlier contained a fluffernutter he had eaten for lunch. It was still covered with the drying blood. He placed it at the base of the old hanging tree. Then he went home.

His day was normal after that. He had a hard time sleeping, but must have dozed off because he woke up at 11:48 that night to the sound of a loud voice booming in his head.

Come to me, it demanded. He got out of bed and dressed. It was time for his first lesson.

Someone was shaking him.

"Honey, it's time for dinner. You gotta wake up from your nap, Frank."

He sat up and shook the sleep from his head.

"What are we having, pumpkin?"

"It's hamburger steaks and mashed potatoes."

"My favorite. I sure love you."

Chapter 12
New Wolf Order

Josh lay on his bed. He had just woken up after sleeping a full ten hours. It was 4:30 in the afternoon. Tess had been blasting Morbid Angel in the next room, in a not too subtle attempt to rise him. *Let the children come to me*, he thought.

He had not gone to school today. He didn't think he would be going anymore. Werewolves learned all they needed to on the streets, or in the woods or something he decided.

He got up and pulled on a pair of jeans and walked out of his room. Tess's room was across the hall and her door was open and he could see her dancing around in the room to the music. She loved to shake it.

"Brother, you're finally up! I've been waiting for so long. What happened last night? Did you turn into a wolf or what? There was like nothing on the tapes!"

"Yeah, I turned into a wolf. I went out, ran around a bit. Some stupid asshole hit me with a stick. Can you believe it? Guess what I did, Tess, guess, guess!" he asked.

"I don't know. You took something he liked and buried it in the yard?"

Josh made a sound like a buzzer on a game show. "That is incorrect Tess, the correct answer is, I bit his fucking head off and drank his blood until he was deeeeeeAAAAAAAAAAD!"

"No way!"

"Way, and you know what else, human blood makes you trip!"

"No way, my girlfriend told me that, and I thought she made it up."

"I had the time of my life last night. This werewolf thing is a good gig. I tell you, things are going to be different around here now."

"Well, I don't know how different things are really gonna be since Mom and Dad are still here. Well, when they're here, that is."

"Don't you see, Tess, Mom and Dad no longer matter. They are obsolete. What the fuck are they gonna do, ground me? No, I don't think so. There's a new head of this household, and it's me. I'm king daddy werewolf and I make the rules."

"So you're saying you were just out last night, walking in the woods, and some guy came up and hit you with a stick? That's so horrible."

"Seriously, what is this town coming to? Augusta is lucky to have me. I'm like fucking Batman cleaning up the streets and shit."

"I can't believe that someone would treat my brother so. I wish I could have bitten their head off."

"Now is the time we should eat all the ice cream," Josh decried, holding up his fist. Tess cheered.

"I love you, brother."

"Don't be gross."

Tess went and got the ice cream from the freezer. There were two boxes. One was vanilla that their father liked and a Moose Tracks for them. She grabbed both boxes and two big spoons.

"I'll take the vanilla now," Josh said, and she passed it over to him.

"Daddy's gonna be mad."

"Aw, fuck him."

Tess giggled and they sat on the couch and watched music videos while eating the ice cream.

"This ice cream's all right, but I need some meat." Josh tossed the melting ice cream box on to the coffee table and walked into the kitchen to find a more suitable snack. He opened the fridge and pulled out a package of raw hamburger. It smelled so good he could not help but lick the blood off the plastic and grab himself a hunk.

He went back in the living room bringing the package with him and watched Tess play video games while he sat reclining in his dad's recliner eating the raw hamburger. He pulled out small chunks, rolled them into little balls, and tossed them into his mouth.

"Oh, my devil brother, what are you doing? Is that even good?"

"Oh yes, Tess, it's chewy and delicious. Here try a piece of it."

"No way, I'll, like, get worms or something."

"Don't be such a pussy, have a bite of hamburger. No one likes a baby that won't eat raw meat."

"Brother, stop talking to me like that, all right. I'll try it! But I'm only doing it because it does look kinda good, and I'm hungry."

"It is good. It's best fresh like this. Cooking takes all the flavor out. I never realized that before, but it's true." Josh passed the Styrofoam burger container over to Tess and she grabbed off a chunk and threw it in her mouth.

"Hey, that is good. It's chewy like gum, but better. It's like meat gum."

"I would never lead you astray, Tess."

"Give me some more of that. It's totally radical!"

Josh was able to hear steps approaching the door.

"Mom's here."

"She is? How do you know?"

"I can hear her on the walkway."

Tess heard the key in the lock and the door swung open to reveal that Josh was right. Their mother was home.

"Told you so," Josh said. Their mother was distracted, walking in the door, because she was carrying a large paper bag. She walked in and set it on the counter and then glanced over to them in the living room.

It would be hard to describe her exact reaction to looking over and seeing her children sitting there in the living room. They had two half melted ice cream containers leaking ice cream all over the coffee table and they were eating raw hamburger from the package she had been planning to use to make spaghetti for dinner. Whenever she thought these two could not surprise her, it turned out she was wrong.

She began shaking and a look of shocked horror trembled on her face for a good two seconds before she began screaming.

"What the fuck are you doing! Stop eating that meat right fucking now! You can't eat raw meat! What is wrong with you? Are you retarded? How could you let your sister eat raw meat?"

"How could you do drugs and drink every night when you were pregnant with us, Mom? Raw meat ain't such a big deal. Brings out the killer instinct."

"I never did that when I was pregnant with either one of you. How dare you say that to me!" his mother shrieked, far beyond livid.

"That's not what Auntie Jill told me, Mom."

"Auntie Jill is a lying whore! I saw her blow a sailor for a black light poster at a carnival. I can't believe you would say that in front of your sister. You know she's sensitive. You should be ashamed."

"No, you should, Mom. We're only what you made us. Mommy's little monsters. Mommy's little monsters!"

She kept on going like she had not even heard him. "That meat was for dinner, and now you've ruined it. Clean up that fucking ice cream now! Listen to me when I'm talking to you. You wait until your father hears about this."

Tess remained silent throughout this. She had seen a lot of bad family fights so she wasn't too scared yet.

"No, you clean it up." Josh had remained calm the whole time and had yet to raise his voice. This was making his mother even crazier with anger.

"WHAT DID YOU SAY?!" she screamed at him.

"You heard me, bitch." She started to take a step forward, and Josh stood up and stared at her with a look of pure hatred and waggled his finger at her. She stepped back alarmed.

"You just wait until you're father hears about this. You'll be sorry then," she shrieked before running into her bedroom and slamming the door shut.

"Holy shit, brother, we are in trouble!" Tess said now able to speak.

"Don't you worry about a thing, little sis, I've got this situation under control. I've always taken care of you. Have faith in your big brother. Like right now I can hear mom. She's calling dad. She also locked the door to her bedroom after she went in, like that would stop me if I wanted in. Dad's going to come home early and deal with this. He's mad at her. He'll be even madder at me when he gets here and then this party will really start."

"Brother, I'm scared. Can you turn into the wolf whenever you want? Are you really gonna eat them?"

"To be honest, I don't quite know what's gonna happen or if I can change at will. It's stimulating."

"It's crazy. Don't let them take you away from me. Promise me, brother. You're all I have."

"Don't worry, Tess, I'll make sure you're taken care of. You have nothing to fear ever again. This is the beginning of a new age for us."

"I don't know anymore. It's starting to seem out of control now. Maybe we should clean up and try to just go back to the way things were. No one has to know about your secret."

"Nothing is controlled. Life is a sea of chaos, girl, you should know better, and as for this current situation, all I can say is objects in motion remain in motion. It's just basic physics. Don't let fear deprive you of your finest moments. They are precious."

Joe Kolgate was seriously pissed off. He had been busy hustling when his wife called him and told him that their children were revolting. He was done with Josh and that kid had it coming bad, for his own good. Joe was damned if his own no-good kids were going to behave this way under his own roof. Well, he would show them who was boss.

He was so angry he stopped at a convenience store to buy himself a tallboy of beer. He drank the pint fast in the car while racing back to his home. If he didn't get this under control soon he might lose his window to re-up and that would mean he would lose money. Joe really hated to lose money, as he never had very much of it.

He drove angrily into the driveway and slammed on the brakes, bringing the car to a screeching halt. He was so full of piss and vinegar he managed to slam the front door both open and closed with one smooth motion. His mouth ripped open like a shotgun blast and he began screaming instantly upon entry.

"WHAT THE FUCK IS GOING ON HERE! TESS YOU CLEAN THAT SHIT UP RIGHT THIS MINUTE AND JOSH YOU COME HERE NOW! YOU NEED TO LEARN RESPECT!"

The room seemed frozen to Tess, and she did not move except for a certain trembling that took over her body. She was not aware of it. She was busy staring in front of her. Josh was walking over to their dad and their mom was coming out of her bedroom.

"You don't get to tell me what to do anymore, old man. It's you that needs to learn respect," Josh said calmly to his father.

Joe did not hesitate. He was in a blind rage now and his fist jabbed forward and cracked Josh straight in the face. Joe was not a big man, but he had at least 80 pounds on the kid.

Josh flew backward onto his back, blood already flowing from his nose, and he got up, spitting more out.

"Is that all you got, old man?" Josh said, and Joe's fist flew again, connecting with his face, knocking him to the ground.

"You see, dad, I'm a werewolf now, and I don't need to take any of your weak ass shit any longer," Josh said while getting up again.

"What you are is an insane person! Well, we'll see how crazy you are in a few minutes, after I beat the crazy out of you." He threw another punch, but this one did not connect. Josh's hand had shot up with wolf-like reflexes and caught the fist and he held it in the palm of his hand.

"I don't think I'm going to let you hit me anymore, Joe. Didn't you listen to me? I said I am a werewolf and you have no power over me anymore." Josh shoved his father backward.

"This house is mine now. Get out. You are not welcome here," Josh said.

"I'll be damned if you're gonna talk to me like that in my own house, boy. I'm gonna beat the crazy out of you." Joe advanced again and swung. No one in the room had eyes that were fast enough to see what happened next.

Josh turned into the wolf and leapt forward, diving into the punch with his mouth open, and bit down, tearing his father's hand off at the wrist. He spun his head to the side, spitting the hand out against the wall. His father fell backward onto the floor, blood spraying from the stump.

"You need to learn some respect, dad," Josh said in a lower than natural voice, and howled up at the rafters.

"This is my house now and you will pay for disrespecting it. You do not deserve life. You shouldn't have been such an asshole, but it's too late now," Josh said, and his father passed out. His mother started screaming and ran for the door.

Josh had reached his limit and swung one huge hairy arm into his mother, throwing her into the wall hard. There was a terrible crashing sound and his mother's head bounced off the wall, cracking like an egg. Josh sat back down on the couch and panted. He was content now.

"Don't worry, Tess, I'm not going to hurt you."

"Brother, you look hot!"

"Thanks."

"Well, what are we gonna do next?"

"I would think that would be fairly obvious, Tess. We're gonna eat our parents."

"Oh, and then what are we gonna do?"

"Then, little sister, we're gonna do whatever we want, whenever we want, forever."

Chapter 13
Game On

Mildred swore that this horrible Tuesday was the longest, most boring day of school in the history of ennui. Ennui had been a vocab word today in English class and it was as fitting as it was cruel.

There were two reasons why the day was taking so long. The first and more exciting, yet also at the same time nerve wracking, reason was that she knew after school they would be playing the game. It was a turn-on and a fear, because she would have to do whatever Trish said. That was part of the rules. Trish had been very excited and close lipped about this despite all of Millie's attempts to get it out of her.

All she would say was that she had been working on this one for a while and it would be, according to her, the best one yet. It was driving Millie crazy, and when the final bell rang, she felt like she was coming and puking at the same time.

She met Trish in the parking lot and they got in the car and began driving home.

"Come on, tell me now. It's time, I know it is," Millie begged.

"Well, I was going to wait until we got back to the house because there is something I have to show you for this to make sense completely. I'm not ready to give it all away yet. This is too good for that. This is kind of a present for you and it cost a lot."

"You're really starting to freak me out, you bitch. Come on, come on."

"All right, well, you know William Blavatski?"

"That AV nerd? What about him?"

"Well, I happened to be sent into the AV room by Miss Hauk on an errand and I caught William watching a very interesting movie. A very explicit movie starring a very prominent member of our high school. He was supposed to be going around catching candid footage for the video yearbook and that creepy brilliant fucker and his zoom lens managed to capture quite an Augusta classic."

"And he just gave it to you? Just like that?"

"No, here's where the cost comes in. I gave him an old fashioned for it."

"Oh, no, a hand job? That's terrible. I'm sorry. You shouldn't have done that."

"You don't know the half of it."

"Was it really that bad?"

"Longest five minutes of my life." They both laughed.

"Horrifying. So who's this video of?"

"You'll see."

"Well, if you whacked William for it, you must have wanted it bad. Hmmm." Millie thought about it in silence, but wasn't able to come up with anyone.

"So, you have this video of this mystery person, what are we gonna do with that?"

"We're gonna blackmail her into doing whatever we want."

"Okay, I'm starting to see where this is going."

It became even more clear when they got home and Trish popped the DVD into the player.

"Holy shit, that's Jessica Drier's house! The fucking homecoming queen bitch bane of my existence, Jessica Drier!" Trish pushed pause.

"That's right. That uptight cunt is ours now. and she's gonna pay, but just watch for now. You have to see this to believe it," Trish said, then hit play again.

The TV showed Jessica's house getting closer and then William suddenly took a detour and started walking around the side of the house. He went up to a large window on the side. He zoomed in and looked around in the house. The lights were on but you still could not see anyone yet. William seemed to give up on this window and zoomed out and continued walking around the side of the house. The camera suddenly got all shaky and they could hear William swear and the sound of a car pulling up.

William went back to the first window and saw Jessica run to the door. She opened it and in came a guy in his mid forties. He threw his arms around her and they began to kiss passionately. William was able to get this though his breathing was starting to get a little heavy. Then they walked out of the frame.

William ran to the next window and caught up with them in the living room. They were kissing, standing up next to a black leather couch. William was able to zoom far in and it was clear exactly who it was and what was going on. All of a sudden Jessica dropped to her knees and ripped open the guy's pants and grabbed his cock.

She started jerking his cock and rubbing it all over her face. William got an extreme close up of this.

"Holy shit, I always knew she was a whore. Too bad there isn't any sound."

"Yeah, sound would have been cool, but it still gets better. Keep watching."

Jessica was sucking his cock now and it was a really big one, but it wasn't fazing her. She was going to town deep throating him, slamming her face off of his belly. This continued for a couple minutes and her makeup started to run. She backed off him and was just jerking the spit lubricated dick with her hand and he shot a huge load out all over the glass coffee table. William was zoomed in close enough to see the semen fly and then Jessica proceeded to lick it up off the table.

"Holy shit! I'm gonna say it again. I mean, holy mother fucking shit!" Millie said.

"That's right, Millie, and your present is on its way."

"What do you mean? What now?"

"In about twenty minutes, Jessica is gonna be arriving here. I told her about the tape and said she could have it back for fifty bucks. But she can't. She's gonna have to work a little harder for that than fifty bucks. For this game you're gonna have to blackmail Jessica into doing whatever we want."

"Blackmail the prom queen. You are a genius! You know all the shit she put me through all through high school. Fucking amazing. I don't know how I'm ever gonna be able to top this. Are you sure she'll do anything we want? I know the video shows she's a total whore, but you think that's enough to make her our slave?"

"It is. That guy in the video lives near me. He's a doctor with three kids. I'm sure she'll play ball. Now let's stay focused on the task at hand. First things first. We play and then later we meet up with Frank."

"I'm so glad school's out. Today is so awesome."

"I take care of you all right, don't I?"

"You're the best friend a girl could have."

"I know, it's not easy, but it is rewarding."

"It sure will be. I'm gonna owe you big for this."

They waited for Jessica to arrive, but that didn't take long. It wasn't more than another ten minutes before the doorbell rang.

"She's early. What a scaredy whore," Trish commented, before going and answering the door.

Jessica stood there in all of her five foot six inch glory. She had long flowing blonde hair that cascaded down her shoulders to a tight pink angora sweater that showed off breasts that seemed too big for such a thin girl. Her body was lean and muscular from cheerleading.

"Come on in, Jessica. You need to see this. We are so worried about you," Trish said.

"Oh, she's here too, huh? I should have known. How about I just give you the fifty bucks, please, and we can just get this over with."

"If I were you, I wouldn't be so bossy when you have so much on the line, Jessica. A video like this could ruin a girl's whole future. You'd have to move to another state, and who knows what your dad would think."

"Oh my god, you wouldn't do that, would you? Please, no, I'll give you more money. Anything, please," Jessica begged, her pouty lip starting to quiver and tears welling up in her eyes. Her face was red and swollen already and they could tell she had been crying on her way there. Mildred took the cue walked over and stroked Jessica's cheek.

"Hush now, don't worry we wouldn't do that. We're not that cruel. We don't want to ruin your life, even if you gave me a hard time in the past. We're all girlfriends here. We don't want your money. We're not trying to blackmail you. We just want to be your friend. Don't you want to be our friend, Jessica? We can be good friends. Good friends that know how to keep a secret."

"Oh, please, would you really?" Jessica said. She didn't sound totally convinced of their sincerity, however, there was a desperate hope in her voice. She needed this to be over. She would do anything.

They ushered her over to the bear skin rug and sat her down before the empty ash filled fire place.

"You need to see this, honey," Mildred said, sitting next to her and putting her arm around her. She noticed that Jessica's muscles were all tense, and smiled. Trish pushed play on the remote control. Mildred continued stroking Jessica's silken blonde hair as she watched in horror. Jessica started crying again as they watched it.

"Shh, it's okay, no one's gonna hurt you. Everyone does it. Don't worry, Jessica," Mildred continued, wrapping her arms around Jessica like she was comforting her.

"To tell you truth, that video kind of made me horny," Mildred said. She slid her hands to softly cup those big soft D cups of Jessica's.

"No, please, I'm not like that, please, anything else." Jessica said, squirming and gently pushing Millie's hands away.

"Now that doesn't seem very friendly to me. Does that seem like how a friend should act to you, Trish?" Millie snarled.

"No, it certainly doesn't. You'd think she'd be more grateful that we were trying to help her," Trish answered.

"Maybe she doesn't want our help."

"No, please, I do want your help," Jessica whispered, another tear rolling down her cheek.

"Then you don't mind if I do this," Millie said, becoming quite aroused by the show of resistance. She eased her hands up to grope those fuzzy pink breasts again.

"Do you have to do that? Isn't there some other way? It's so unnatural. It's not right for a girl to touch another girl like that. It's . . . it's a sin!" Jessica said, her body shaking as she allowed Millie to feel and squeeze her breasts.

Millie pinched Jessica's now rock hard nipple and slapped her hard across the face.

"Don't say that shit to me. I'm trying to be your friend. Do you want me to send that tape to your parents and the whole school? I'm sure they'd love to see what a nasty cum slut the prom queen and head cheerleader is. It would reinforce all of their precious fantasies."

"No, please, I'll do anything else, just don't make me do that. It's against God."

"Well, listen to me, you little slut, we don't care what God thinks in this house, and if you really cared what he thought you wouldn't be whoring around sucking and fucking like you clearly are, so can that hypocritical bullshit before I get really mad. But we aren't going to make you do anything. If you'd rather have us send the video to your parents, and the whole school. I'm sure that could be arranged. Oh, and let's not forget your precious church. I'm sure Rev Petafye would love to see what a dirty whore his precious choir angel is."

"He'd probably give you a solo," Trish added.

"No, no, please, I'll be good," Jessica begged. Mildred started feeling her up again, this time slipping her hands up underneath the sweater and feeling those soft globes again.

"These are nice. Come over her, Trish, and feel the prom queen's titties. Hold your arms up like a good girl, Jessica," Millie said.

Jessica did as she said and Millie pulled off the tight sweater and the shirt in one smooth motion.

This left Jessica standing there in a pink and white bra with ruffles and a black skirt and pumps. Millie opened the front clasp on the bra and her breasts popped free.

"Wow! That is a great pair of tits, and look at these, you could cut glass with 'em, I think she likes this," Trish said, latching on and sucking one of the nipples. Jessica started to make a face at first but Millie cut her off with a sharp look.

"I'm not going to try and convince you to be good again, you got it?" Millie said.

"I got it, Millie. I'll be good, I promise."

Millie pushed her back down onto the fur, stood up, and stripped off her top. She leaned over and put her breast in Jessica's face. She reached her hand behind Jessica's hesitant head and eased it toward her breast. Jessica gently began to suck it.

"That's my good girl. Yeah, do it like that," Millie said as Jessica suckled. She looked over at Trish and they grinned at each other. Millie held up her hand and they high-fived. Trish took off her clothes and sat down wearing only an ear to ear grin. Millie had Jessica suck on Trish's pink nipples as she got naked.

Jessica was still wearing her skirt and a black thong. Millie came up to her from behind and pulled down the panties. Jessica's body tensed up but she did not resist. Her will was broken. She flinched but did not say anything as she felt Millie's cool hand slide up her thigh all the way to her pussy.

"You're all shaved. What a whore. You know how I can tell you're a whore? You act all prissy like this is something new for you, but your slut pussy is as wet as Niagara Falls. You love sucking her tits, and now you're gonna love licking my cunt until I come all over that pretty prom queen face of yours," Millie said, and laid back spreading her legs wide.

She motioned with one finger to draw Jessica to her and grabbed the prom queen by her blonde hair as soon as she was close enough and roughly pushed her face between her legs. Jessica was stunned, her face only an inch or so away from Mildred's wet pussy. She could smell her vile desire.

"Are you looking for another slap? Is that like your deal, you need to be punished? Lick it, bitch!"

Jessica opened her mouth and began tentatively licking with her eyes closed. She started to gag for a second but kept on going. Mildred moaned and began to grind her pussy into Jessica's face. Trish started fingering Jessica's sopping wet dream box.

"You're right, Millie, it's like a water park down here. I think you might be a dyke, Jessica. We won't tell, though. It'll just be another one of our little secrets."

Eventually after several orgasms, Millie had had enough and set Jessica to work on Trish.

"I don't think she's trying hard enough," Trish said. Millie reared back and slapped Jessica's ass, leaving a bright red hand print on the milky white derriere.

"You better get her off or I'm gonna go get my strap-on and fuck you in the ass. You hear me, Jessica? You eat that pussy right, or else it's your ass!" Jessica's eyes screamed and she began furiously going to town on Trish. Trish came loudly soon thereafter.

"Well, I guess you're off the hook this time. Now get your clothes and get the fuck out," Millie said. Jessica started to dress.

"Don't forget who your friends are, Jessica," Trish said, spanking her hard on the ass again. "That's one to grow on."

"I won't," she said softly, with a shameful red face.

"You know what. I don't think that's good enough," Trish said, and reached into her purse. She pulled out a high powered electric stun gun and pressed it to Jessica's neck. She pressed in hard and pulled the trigger on the highest setting.

The small girl dropped to the ground, shaking and drooling.

"What do you think, Millie? I'll leave it up to you. Should we let her go or drag her out back?"

"FUCK it, I'm still so fucking horny. Let's take her out back," Mildred said.

Trish shocked the prone girl again and they both dragged her out the front door and around the back of the house. There was no one around for miles so they weren't worried about witnesses. Trish ran to the garage and came back with her bowie knife.

"What do you think, Millie? Do you mind if I chop this cunt up for kicks, or do you want to?"

"You can, but wait. Wait a second," Mildred said. She and Trish were still naked and Jessica was wearing her bra and panties. Millie was furiously rubbing her clit, standing up, shaking and moaning at the sight of the nude Trish with the blade standing over Jessica.

"Yes, honey, tell mama what you want, baby," Trish said.

"Oh, Trish, please, please . . . pee on her. Oh, please, for me. Do it for me," Millie moaned.

"Is that what baby wants?" Trish said. Millie just nodded. Jessica was just starting to stir as Trish stood over her head.

"You can do it, mama, come on," Millie said to cheer her on, and it seemed to work as the pee started to flow onto Jessica's face, who spit and gagged and begged for them to let her go.

"NOW NOW NOW!" Mildred screamed, and Trish swung the knife down again and again, stabbing Jessica to death as Millie punctuated each of her orgasms by calling out a different demon's name.

Chapter 14
Get Your Gun

Frank woke up at 4:30 on the next day. He wasn't sure how to proceed. Was it all some sort of bizarre dream or hallucination?

"Josette, are you there?" he called, feeling awkward, but she appeared smiling in front of him. He wasn't sure if that was a good thing or a bad thing.

"Good morning, or afternoon I should say. Are you ready to go kill or would you like some breakfast first?" she said, her child face was kind of creepy, but in a good way Frank thought.

"Um, I think I'll be starting with the breakfast, then, uh, I guess I'll be moving on to the human sacrifice," Frank said. He was nervous. He'd never killed anyone before. He certainly didn't want to go to jail.

Frank walked through the computer room, on through the living room, and into the kitchen where he popped an onion bagel into the toaster. He smeared on some butter and then veggie cream cheese on top, making it decadent.

I need to find a gun today. He was supposed to meet up with those girls today too. It was going to be a busy day. Maybe they could help me. After all, Millie had robbed that store.

He trusted these girls enough to help him find a piece if they could, but he wouldn't tell them about what he was gonna do with it. That would just be stupid. He knew it was most peoples' big stupid wagging mouths that got them into trouble and he was going to try to avoid that. I hope this apocalypse thing pans out and I won't have to worry about imaginary things like laws anymore.

Nayte walked in the front door with his bass slung over his shoulder in a black gig bag. He was wearing a Crimson Ghosts "Walk Don't Run Among Us" t-shirt.

"Hey, dude, how was practice?" Frank called.

"Eh, it was okay. Hey, you killed that woman yesterday didn't you? I read about it in today's Kennebec Journal."

"No, I think I'd remember that. What are you talking about?"

"There was another fire. A house burned down in town and there was a woman in it this time. I figured it must have been you since you burned down that church."

"No, that one wasn't me. Must have been some other asshole," Frank said and then to be hospitable added, "Care for a bagel?"

"No way, man. Carbs are poison," Nayte said, and fired up the red plastic bong. It had a crooked sticker that had been peeled off some other product and stuck onto it that read "safe for all ages." He passed the bong to Frank, who walked into the living room brushing the bagel crumbs off his shirt. Frank took a "clear his head and prepare for the day" bong hit.

"Man, things have been really weird lately. Am I going fucking crazy or what, dude?" Frank said, taking a seat on the couch.

"Dude, you're like the sanest guy I know, who cares, man?"

"Yesterday I saw a little dead girl rise up from a grave and she's been talking to me ever since."

"Is that all, Frank? I see shit like that all the time and don't even care. That's not real, nothing to worry about. Remember all that acid we did? Well, you know, maybe that has something to do with it. Who knows, guy, I'm just saying."

"This is not an acid flashback. I'm not even sure I believe in those."

"Don't kid yourself. They are very much realer than you think. Didn't you think you were having one once?"

"Yeah, maybe, but I don't know really. I had an uncle that did a lot of acid in the 60's and never had a flashback. Either way this is beyond that, I don't know, fuck it."

"It's not worth getting stressed over, man."

"Oh, I know, fuck it. Conversely, things could be worse, though. I am going to be in the company of two smoking hot girls shortly, one of which was kind hearted enough to let me sodomize her whenst last we met."

"Well, that sounds pretty snap ass to me."

He wanted to tell Nayte about Jack Valenti, but it was too dangerous. Frank trusted him, and he'd probably help if he needed it, but some things are best done alone. They smoked more pot and everything was normal again.

He got up. It was time to call the girls, he reckoned. He dialed the number on the caller id from Mildred. She and Trish were in town. He told them he'd be walking up Water St. and they agreed to come and pick him up. He bid Nayte farewell and headed out on his quest. His exit card was major arcana sixteen, The Tower.

Frank pondered the card as he walked up the road. Marijuana was good for this kind of thinking. The tower showed ambition and fighting. It could mean courage as well, but it could also sometimes mean destruction or ruin. Much like the attributes of the card itself. *It must be about balance*, he thought, *just got to be tower enough, but not too much tower or I'll screw myself over.* He looked at the number sixteen for further analysis.

He knew sixteen was considered by some to be a number of karmic debt and ego related, but also from the other side it was the number of Abra-melin and the servitors of Asmodee. He decided it was a good sign. He would be better prepared for this reddish work keeping that in mind. Too many people just viewed the Tarot as a future telling method instead of using it to remind one of different ways of seeing a situation to increase the likelihood of impacting one's will on one's surroundings.

It came to him all of a sudden that he knew where there might be a gun, and he smiled. It was too perfect.

He saw the familiar crime-mobile pull to the side of the road.

"The bell rings time for deja vu, ladies, how's it going today?" Frank said, getting in the back seat. He noticed the girls had a smug look about them.

Trish turned around and kissed him full on the mouth.

"That's how I am, Frank," Trish said, breaking the kiss with a crooked half smile.

"We're pretty good today, Frank. It's nice to see you again so soon," Millie said. "Satan loves you, Frank."

"Yeah, I know. The feeling's mutual."

"So what do you feel like doing, Frank, wanna go get a hot dog or something?" Trish said.

"Yeah, I could go for a hot dog or two. That sounds groovy. So you're feeling talkative today, Trish," Frank said.

"I try and mix it up," she said. They drove to the hot dog shack and got six hot dogs with sauerkraut and mustard. It came to eleven ninety-three. They sat on top of a faded red picnic table eating the savory treats.

"I'm in a bit of a pickle girls. I need a ride over to this camp so I can get a heater."

"A heater? What's that?"

"What, you never read The Outsiders? It's a gun and I need one. Can you help out a friend in need?" he said.

"Of course we'll help you, Frankie, what are friends for?" Trish said.

"Thanks, that really means a lot to me," Frank replied.

"How soon do you need it?" Trish asked.

"As soon as possible. Tonight would really be best. Someone could be coming for me."

He gave them directions to Disco's camp. It wasn't far from there. He hoped Jack Valenti's gun was still there.

"Whose car is this anyway?" Frank asked.

"It's mine," Trish said.

"I just drive it sometimes," Millie said.

"It's cool. So what did you want to talk to me about?"

"Well, Frank, it's kind of like this, there are two kinds of people in the world, you dig. People like them and people like us. Most people are like them, but you, however, are like us. Do you know what I mean?" Trish said.

"Yeah, I know what you mean, but I'm not sure what you're getting at."

"What she's getting at is that you're not alone now, Frank. You are with friends—friends who would never dessert you. You need a gun, and we will put a gun right in your hand. It's nothing. We want to know you better, and we are not alone, Frankie. It's a big, big world."

"Thanks. I'm grateful to meet such friendly friends, and if this doesn't work out, I might take you up on that," Frank said.

"I'm too sober to be explaining this right. It's not normally what we do. Millie pack a bowl, pretty please, maybe that will help. It really should be my Daddy talking to you now," Trish said, with an enigmatic laugh.

"You'll like him, Frank . . . everybody does," Millie added.

"The thing is, he's out of town on business right now, but he'll be back tomorrow," Trish said. They started passing the glass pipe around the car.

"Nice piece," he said, admiring the hand blown color changing glass.

"I've heard that one before," Millie said with a smile. They were stoned to the gills by the time they reached the camp with Kilslug blasting their sludgey gospel of hate through the speakers as they tore down the old country roads. These girls really have amazing taste in music for their age, Frank thought. Three cheers for the Internet.

"Wait here, girls, and keep the motor running," Frank said, and hopped out of the car. He ran up and lifted the turtle. Jackpot. The key was still there.

Frank unlocked the door of the cabin and went inside. He flipped on the light and jumped, expecting a figure to rise out of the blackness, but none did.

"Come on luck don't fail me now," Frank mumbled.

He dropped to his hands and knees and looked under the cot in the corner. Royal flush!

Just like he remembered it, he saw the .357 revolver, which when he had last seen had been in Disco's mouth. The presence of the gun made it all real, and he let out a shuddery breath. Action time. He reached out and grabbed the gun. It felt sexy in his hand. He took off his zippered hoodie. He made sure the safety was on the gun and wrapped it in the sweatshirt. He turned off the light and locked the door behind him, leaving the key under the turtle as he had found it. He walked over to the car and got in.

"You find what you were looking for?" Millie asked.

"Yeah I did, Millie," Frank said, unfolding the sweatshirt and holding the gun out between the two front seats. The girls moaned at the sudden appearance of the big gun.

"What do you ladies want to do now?" Frank asked.

"Let's go back to my house and chill," Trish said. It sounded good to all of them and they sped out to Windsor.

Once they were there they led him into the living room.

"I'm going to go change. Why don't you make our guest more comfortable," Millie said, taking off down a dark corridor.

"More comfortable. That sounds good," Frank said.

"Oh yeah, are you horny, baby? Want a hand job?" she said, pantomiming jerking off and smiling.

"I have a strict acceptance policy on that kind of responsible behavior." He didn't want to appear rude.

"Come with me then," she said and took him by the hand.

"Oh, I will."

She led him into a bathroom, but left the door open. She undid his pants and got the reaction she was going for. She grabbed a bottle of lemon meringue scented hand lotion and squirted a healthy glob into her palm.

He obliged by opening his pants and his prick popped out from the hole in his argyle boxers. She made a happy sound like a duck deep in her throat and grabbed his cock with those slender slippery hands, pulling and stroking it to maximum stiffness. He let out a little moan as she continued to jerk him off while staring deep into his eyes.

"Smells like I'm fucking a pie, but it does feel so goooood," Frank confessed. She giggled but did not miss a stroke.

"Well, he definitely looks more comfortable now," Millie said, walking up to the bathroom with a blunt in one hand and a pistol in the other, an angry look on her face.

Seeing her watching almost made him shoot, but he held back, not done with this scene yet. Millie walked up and pressed her lips against his, giving him a huge shotgun hit. He held it in for what seemed like five minutes. It was good stuff and he was baked by the time he exhaled. Millie slipped one of her tiny hands up the back of his neck and caressed it.

"It's all right, Frankie, you can let go, baby," she breathed into his ear, licking up the lobe.

"Make him come or I'll blow your fucking brains out, whore," Millie said, raising the gun and pressing it to Trish's face. Trish jerked him off but he noticed her other hand up under her plaid skirt.

"You know you're mine, don't you?" Millie said.

"I know," Frank said.

Millie pushed the barrel harder against Trish's head. Trish's hand went into overdrive.

"You deserve to die, you fucking dirty little slut. You're fuckin' filthy," Millie said in a fierce voice. Trish's breath was coming in little whimper moans, but she still managed to turn her head and started fellating the barrel of the gun.

It was a little too much for Frank and he lost control and started coming in Trish's face. She was screaming her own bliss, partially muffled by the gun barrel in her mouth with warm come running down her cheek like salty crocodile tears. Millie pulled the trigger and the gun clicked.

"Bang," she whispered.

Trish fell over spent onto the bathroom floor. Millie reached out and stroked Frank's cheek while making eye contact with him. Her eyes never left his as she dropped to her knees and paused for a second before licking Trish's cheek clean with one lick of her long freakish tongue.

"Fuck, yeah!" Frank yelled and almost fell over.

"That was fucking hot," Millie said.

Trish was too discombobulated to say anything.

"That was ridiculously sexy," he agreed, taking the blunt from Millie. He took a moderate sized hit and passed it to the "dead" girl on the floor. She was resurrected by the drug.

"Puff, puff, pass motherfucker! Oh my fucking devil, I just came so fucking hard I had an out of body experience," Trish said, exhaling a huge smoke ring and struggling to rise from the tile floor.

Frank, feeling a sense of chivalry helped her rise to her feet, and then noticed his cock was still hanging out. He tucked it back into his jeans and zipped up.

"You showing me yours made me want to play with mine," Millie said. She pointed at his gun. "Be careful with that thing, Frankie, we need you around."

"I wouldn't worry about me, ladies. I'm a man that can take care of myself," Frank said, reassuring himself as well as the girls. *I will take care of myself and I'll take care of that fucking Jack Valenti cocksucker too.* He stared at the gun in Millie's hand and smiled.

"It's not as big as yours, but I think it's stylish," she said.

"It suits you quite well," Frank said. "Brings out your eyes."

The gun was going to make this a whole lot easier. He didn't know if he could have done it without a gun. He didn't think he could take Valenti in a physical contest, but now they'd be on even ground. He had the great equalizer and the will to equalize.

"You two are not like anyone I've ever met before, and I've met some of the weirdest motherfuckers you're ever likely to meet."

"Be still my beating heart, is that a post orgasm compliment I hear?" Millie said.

"I give credit where credit is due, and you girls got it going on. I thank the lord Satan to even be in the room with you. Maybe we do have great things to accomplish together."

"Don't doubt it for a minute, handsome. I mean what are the odds we'd even make it this far," Millie said, smiling at him. She had a smile that touched him somewhere.

"Are you sure there's nothing we could do to help you, Frank? You could stay here if people are looking for you. There's no need for you to do anything rash to protect yourself."

"No, no, you have done plenty already, sweet face. As proof, I really trust you girls, I will tell you I am going to use this gun to kill a man. It must be done. It's killing time for assholes."

"Aw. Sweetie, that's so cute. It kinda makes me want to fuck you," Mildred said.

"Don't worry, it's easy, Frankie. We'll totally help you with this. There are options available to a man like you," Trish said.

"That's sweet of you, but no. This is something I have to do myself," Frank said.

"My little boy is gonna be all grown up soon," Trish said and smiled.

"So you two sex crazed teens are blood thirsty killers? You expect me to believe that?" Frank said.

"Honey, I killed two people this week," Trish said. "How's that for trust?"

"Prove it," Frank said.

"Think he can handle going downstairs, Millie?" Trish said.

"Yeah, I think he's ready for it."

"Alright. Now this is a big secret Frank. Daddy would be so pissed if he knew we were showing you this, but you did burn the church, and I know he'd show you himself if he knew you. The reason why we're ahead of the curve, Frank, is we've been grandfathered in. I was born with my name in the black book, Frank. Come with me," Trish said, and opened a door off the living room that opened to a dark rickety stair case.

Trish flipped the switch and one dim bulb lit up down in the basement. She led them down to the dirt floored basement. They walked all the way across it and came to a large metal door with three huge padlocks on it.

"We got a little crazy yesterday and I killed the prom queen with my bowie knife. I stabbed her up pretty good and we brought her down here. She's right behind this door if you want to get a piece. This is Daddy's crematorium," Trish said, pulling a chain up out of her shirt with three keys on it.

"For real?" Frank said. He was starting to believe, but it was shocking.

"Yes, Frank. I've only killed three people, and Jessica was the only one for pleasure," Trish said while unlocking the padlocks from top to bottom.

"We haven't burned the body yet, Frank. We've been playing with it," Millie said smiling.

"So um . . . why the fuck does your dad have a crematorium in the basement?"

"Daddy bought this house because it used to be an old funeral home. We just live in it now, but daddy sometimes operates a freelance cremation business."

"That is quite amazing."

"Oh, the fun never stops around here."

The door was completely unlocked now, but Trish did not open it. She turned around and looked at Frank.

"You sure you're ready to play with the big boys, Frank? You don't have to come in here."

"I can take it darling," Frank said.

With that Trish whipped open the door and stepped inside.

"Come on in," She said. "I made it witchy for you, Charlie."

Frank walked in and smelled. She had been telling the truth. The room was empty except for a gurney with a blue tarp on it. The oven was at the far side. There were metal lockers covering the walls. The only decoration was a velvet painting of Elvis with a headless and topless girl and a palm tree.

Frank walked right over to the gurney. The girls unfolded the tarp and he saw Jessica's hacked up naked body.

"Woah . . . she's beautiful," Frank said.

"We burned her clothes already. You can fuck her if you want, Frank, I won't mind. I'm not the jealous type. Some people like that sort of thing. We fucked her before I killed her," Trish said.

"Wow . . . that's . . . intense." Frank said, staring at the body. "I want to, but I'm not sure I could. The smell is putting me off."

"Please, baby do it for me."

Trish snuggled up to him. She put her hand on his crotch and kissed him. She felt his cock move through his pants and dropped to her knees. His cock's flaccid state did not have a chance.

Trish stopped long enough to tell Millie to put Jessica on the floor for Frank. Trish tipped the gurney and Jessica's body and the tarp tumbled off.

Millie flattened out the tarp and positioned Jessica in the middle. She had to pull hard, but she managed to spread the corpse's legs.

"You ready to fuck the prom queen, Frankie?" Millie asked.

"Her face and tits are pretty hacked up. Why don't you flip her over for me?" Frank requested.

Millie did as he asked.

"Yeah, that's much better. I think I'm ready," Frank said, pulling his very stiff cock out of Trish's greedy mouth. She gave a little whimper of sadness as it left her lips, but then she remembered the plan.

Frank walked over to the tarp on the floor.

"Wait, Frank!" Millie said, and ran up to him. She pulled a condom out of her purse and gave it to him. "Be safe, Frankie, be safe."

"Good thinking, doll. I don't want to get dick rot. Put it on for me," Frank said.

Millie looked over at Trish, who nodded. She blushed and opened the condom, pinching the air out of the tip, and slowly rolled it down Frank's cock, careful to touch only the condom.

"Yeah, baby," Frank said, winking at her, and then penetrated Jessica from behind.

Millie walked around so she was facing Frank, looking him in the eye as he made love to Jessica. She pulled up her skirt and snapped her fingers. Trish dropped to her knees and began to tongue her. That made Frank kick it up to high gear and he started giving it all he had as hard as he could. Millie shrieked out a mighty orgasm, but Trish didn't stop. Millie screamed again and slapped Trish across the face. Trish finally let her go just as Frank lost his cool. He withdrew and the room was quiet. Panting, with the stink of death hanging heavy in the air.

"Well, that was pretty fucking weird . . . let's go back upstairs and smoke some more weed,"

Frank said. They wrapped the tarp around Jessica's body and lifted her back onto the gurney.

Trish shut the door behind them and fastened the three huge locks. They went upstairs and smoked to get rid of the smell of death.

They hung out there and drank some beers and listened to the Dwarves. The refrain—two things that drive me insane, teenage women and free cocaine—kept repeating in his head. It was a good time and in the midst of the celebration Frank realized who he needed to see for the only other help he would need: Spider. Spider was the hardest guy he knew. The guy was awesome at crime. He might not have a crematorium in his basement, but he would be able to offer assistance of a more practical nature, Frank was certain. Plus he missed the guy, who had done a lot of time on and off.

Chapter 15
Spider helps out

Frank had the girls drive him back to town and drop him off on an adjacent street and then he walked the rest of the way to Spider's apartment. He had the gun under his hoodie.

He walked the three blocks up and turned a right onto Spider's street. He hoped Spider was fucking home. He felt weird walking around with the gun, like somehow people would know he had it on him, like a sign was lit up over his head. He was very aware of its weight against his chest. *If I'm ever gonna make any headway here, I'm going to need to get rid of this terrible paranoia.* Thinking that cleared his head.

He continued up the narrow walkway and entered the outside door of the apartment building. He climbed the decrepit old staircase and knocked on the door with the three on it. He could hear some kind of extreme metal being played from the hallway, but couldn't make out the band. The music turned down.

"It's me, Spider, open up, man," Frank called. The door opened and Spider was standing there. He was wearing a pair of black military combat pants. He stood a little over six feet and was heavily muscled and tattooed. He had slicked back black hair.

"Hey, Frankie, come on in," he said.

Frank entered the apartment. It was a small, cheap place in a crumby building, but Spider had the place packed with nice stuff inside. He also noticed Spider had added a lot of strange art hanging on the walls.

"Wow, what's that? It's amazing."

"That's The Garden of Earthly Delights, painted by Hieronymus Bosch in the fifteenth century. He's a recent obsession of mine."

"You are a complex person, Spider."

"Thanks. What do you need?"

"I'm in a little bit of a tight spot here. I need a car to get around in for a little bit—something not too traceable, you know what I mean?"

"Yeah, I know what you mean," he said.

"So do you think I could maybe rent a car like that off you or something?"

"Rent? That's a laugh. You don't have shit. I can't just let you take a car. It doesn't work that way."

"I know it's a favor, but I'll owe you big, man. There's got to be something I can do for you?"

"You taking a car and going off by yourself, that ain't a favor, that's suicide, but I will do you a favor. I'll drive you. That's me, doing you, a favor."

"It's real heavy shit, man. You're better off not involved or knowing anything. I'm looking to find somebody you might know," Frank said, and opened his sweatshirt to show he was carrying.

"Know how fucking well, because there are some names you do not want to be uttering next," Spider said, his voice tightening with hostility.

"Valenti."

"I don't know that guy. Fuck that asshole, he ain't nothing to me. So like I said, I'll give you a ride. It ain't no big thing."

"You're sure you want to go along for this?"

"Who the fuck do you think you're talking to, man, Pope Fucking Justice the sixth? I don't give a shit if you're going to go burn down a fucking orphanage and then cornhole Santa. No one drives one of my cars except me. You got it, mate?"

"OK, I got it."

"You got a plan too?"

"I heard he hangs out down at Richard's Lounge. I was going to check and see if he was out that way and then follow him to wherever he goes. Keep going up the road, or whatever, then creep back down and take care of business. Just keep it simple, you know."

"That's as good a place as any to start, but let me see if I can pull his info up on the computer," Spider said, and walked over to the fancy rig set up in the corner.

"I hate this computer shit, man, but I had to learn how to do it myself so I don't have to rely on some geek to keep his fucking mouth shut. It's amazing the things you can learn in the can," Spider said, sitting down and typing away. Spider paused and turned to him. "There ain't nothing in this world fucking worse than a rat, Frankie."

"I'd have to agree, man."

"Dead Jesus yes," Spider said.

Frank watched Spider's fingers flying over the keys.

"Impressive. I couldn't do that," Frank said.

"That's just because you've never had to before. You'd be amazed at the things you can learn to save your ass. Not that it really fucking matters much now. The whole fucking planet is going to hell in a big old way and it is good for business, my friend. I guarantee if this was ten years ago, I'd be in prison again for the shit I been into. But the strangler is here to save us all. Patron saint of criminals. All us lower and middle level guys are getting a pass right now."

"That is very good to hear." Frank laughed, then stood still as Spider kept working.

A couple of minutes later Spider let out a triumphant call.

"I got it from the DMV, that fucker rolls around in a red 1965 mustang. I got his address too," Spider said.

"I knew this was the right place to go."

Spider laughed at that.

"We're going to have us a real wild night, Frankie."

"What time is it, Spider?"

"It's just about ten o'clock."

"It might be too early for him to be at the bar, so I say if he's not there, we go by his house and case that place out as best we can, unless you have a better idea?"

"This is your baby. Go with it. It's all instinct. Animal nature. First, though, we need to pick up the car."

"Oh yeah?"

"You think I'd have the kind of car we could go do something like that in parked out front? This ain't amateur hour here. Start using your head."

"Okay, okay."

"Don't worry, there's nothing to it, it's all common sense. If I was worried about it, I wouldn't help you," Spider said, and hearing that from him did make Frank feel better.

Spider smacked Frank on the shoulder.

"Come on, let's go get that cherry of yours busted," he said. He grabbed a bible off the shelf and opened it. It had been hollowed out and there was a snub nose revolver in it. He put in the inside pocket of his leather jacket.

"You're the best, man. Everyone should have a friend like you," Frank said.

Sometimes friends do come through for you. His luck was getting better and better as the day went on, it seemed. He was feeling confident now. The smoke was starting to wear off and he could feel himself getting more aware, and he was feeling more powerful. He was ready to go out and kill a man.

They went out and got in Spider's nondescript brown four door and headed out of town and into the woods of Rome.

After another fifteen minutes of driving back roads, they reached a junkyard at the end of a very long driveway. There was a sign on the tall fence that said Red's Junkyard. The gate was padlocked shut. Spider parked in front of it and got out of the car. He walked over and opened the lock with a key off his bondage belt and slid the gate open with a shove from his powerful arms.

He came back to the car and they drove in, parking in front of a large garage.

"Follow me," he said, leading Frank behind the garage where a bunch of cars were parked. He pointed to a row of five of them and said to pick one of those. Frank picked a blue Corsica. They got in the car and drove out the gate. Spider stopped to shut and lock the gate behind them.

They drove back into town to Richard's Lounge. It was located on Augusta's scenic waterfront. There was a classical station softly playing Black Aria. Frank felt good.

They cruised down into the parking lot of the lounge and drove around, but there was no Mustang to be found.

"Guess it might have been a long shot that he'd be here now, but no matter, let's go find where this guy lives," Frank said.

They drove out of there and stopped at a convenience store so Spider could grab a cup of coffee. Frank gave him a couple dollars to grab him an energy drink. He cracked the lid and guzzled a shot of the stuff.

"Mmm, taste that taurine flavor," he said.

"I stick with the coffee myself. That taurine, man, I heard it's bull semen."

"That sounds kind of hard to believe, but maybe that's why they are so expensive. Bull semen probably makes you strong anyway."

"Hey, if you turn into a cow fag, don't say I didn't warn you."

"Duly noted for the record."

They continued on with the murder business and jetted out to the address. It was a dark house. There were no lights on and no car parked in front of it, Frank noticed as they passed it. Spider continued driving until he saw the next driveway about five hundred yards down the road. He pulled in, and thankfully no one was home here either. He killed the lights and the engine.

"Go and check it out. I'll wait here for you," Spider said. He also gave Frank the number of his latest disposable cell phone. Frank got out and walked back to the road and headed to Valenti's house. He got prepared for murder just in case. He pulled the gun out of his hoodie as he bolted up the driveway, keeping it under his coat, but in his hand as well. He flipped the safety off as he reached the door and rang the bell.

"Josette, go and see if anyone's home," he said, clutching the gun tight in his hand.

She flew out of his ring and through the door. His heart was racing and everything seemed to be going in slow motion. It was a very intense moment standing there in the dark with a gun in his hand and murder on his mind. Any moment Valenti could open the door and he was ready to put one in his face the second that happened. He couldn't hear any sounds coming from the house whatsoever. He waited and waited.

"It's empty," Josette's spectral voice called.

He decided to enter and tried the door, but it was locked. That was unusual for an isolated house like this one in Maine, but people like Valenti always locked their doors. There was always a reason, and today it was Frank.

There was nothing useful around the side of the house, but there was a big red porch on the back. There was a large grill on the deck and it was connected to the house via two large glass sliding doors. They were also locked.

Fuck it, he thought, *you gotta have balls some time,* and he holstered his gun. He grabbed the grill and put it through the glass door in one sudden and violent motion. It was loud for a split second, then quiet again. He wasted no time, and shook the grill around enough to make a big enough hole for him to get through. The propane tank went spinning off across the kitchen floor and rolled against an easy chair. He entered the house and found a light and turned it on.

The place was pretty clean, with the exception of the floor being covered with shards of glass and grill accessories. He flinched from an immense clown in a lurid pose, but it just turned out to be a very creepy and extremely large painting. He looked around a few more minutes and then pulled out his cell phone and called Spider.

"Hey, man, I'm inside, and I think I'll just stay here and wait for him. How about I call you later and you can come back to where you are now and pick me up."

"Are you sure that's what you want to do?" Spider asked.

"Yeah, it's the right plan."

"Okay, call me later," Spider said, and hung up.

Frank moved a kitchen chair to sit with a clear view of the front door and turned off all the lights and waited for his victim.

Chapter 16
The Pied Piper Kills a Family

Josh was sitting on the couch munching on leftovers. It turned out two adults made an awful lot of tasty chow. He made Tess clean the place up pretty good, and they were enjoying their new found freedom. Searching his parents' room, he found half a pound of marijuana and fifteen hundred dollars in cash. That made things a little easier for them. *I should have killed them years ago. This is the proper way to live.*

He and Tess had been on this cycle of smoking pot and getting the munchies and eating more of their parents for the last day, broken up with spurts of video games, TV, and napping. Everything was going fine, but Tess started begging for him to turn back into the wolf again. He wanted to see if he could do it at will anyway, so he tried and it worked.

Tess cheered and bounced on the couch. Josh the wolf looked at her once, then ran out of the house. The darkness was soothing to him after the horrible brightness of the house.

He hadn't meant to run, but he was no longer in control of his faculties. He was operating on some kind of autopilot and he was running somewhere in a hurry. *This can't be good.* He wondered where he was running to.

It was like watching some kind of twisted reality TV show. He was running so fast the trees and house were a blur to him. He saw a house up ahead in a row of similar houses and he knew that was where he was going as soon as it came into sight.

The strangler knew the wolf was coming the minute it transformed and he leapt out of bed. He had been waiting for this.

He thought it might get loud and weird when the wolf showed up. His wife stirred a little when he got out of bed but didn't wake.

Better safe than sorry, he thought and reached into the bedside table and withdrew a syringe hidden beneath a false bottom. He filled it and jabbed it into his wife's arm. She cried out, but just for a second before rolling over and falling back asleep.

"That's it, rest now, dear, you've earned it," he said and kissed her forehead. He slipped his robe over his crimson pajamas. He went downstairs to await the arrival of the wolf.

Josh was starting to freak out a little, but there was nothing he could do but watch as he ran. Was this the way it would always be from now on? Was the wolf taking over now, finally? Isn't

176

that just the way things always are? There has to be a catch to everything, right? He approached the door to the house. It opened when he was about five feet from it.

There was a very normal looking man standing there with a big smile on his face. He looked to be in his forties and had short brown hair. He was nondescript except for the dangerous eyes.

"You're here at last! The boy who lay down with the wolf, made wolf, welcome, welcome, you'd better come into the house before anyone sees you," the man said, motioning for him to enter.

Josh stooped to get through the door frame in his big wolf body and entered the house. They walked forward together into the living room.

"My name is Franklin. What is your name, wolf? Are you a Canadian?" the strangler said.

"Josh is my name, and no, I'm an American. Have you done something to me?"

"I have brought you here tonight, Josh. I wanted to meet you. You are very special indeed and you will help me pass from here to there. Certain things have to happen. All the possibilities must play out. Ah! I can almost remember it already. Open your nose, Josh, and smell. Smell the dawn of the end! It is an exciting time to be alive, Josh, it really is."

"What do you want from me?"

"I will tell you when it is time, and don't be frightened. You will want to help me, and if you don't, you can just walk away. It's your call, Josh."

"Doesn't sound like I have much choice."

"That is only true if you make it true. How old are you Josh?"

"I'm only nineteen. But I guess that's pretty old in dog years."

"I just wanted to say hello, but if you need me call me," Franklin said, and handed him a card with his number on it.

"Yeah, sure. I guess you don't really need mine."

"No, I don't. I'll be seeing you, Josh."

"Later, Franklin."

The killer watched the wolf disappear, racing into the darkness. He stood there wondering how things were going to play out in this town. Rare things were happening here more and more often. The rate at which this was increasing was starting to seem exponential and it interested him. Reality could only take so much. He was determined to push it as far as it could go.

He was trying his best to hasten the end of the world along. He looked forward to it for the spiritual rewards.

He felt frustrated so he decided to go out and kill some people. *First person I see, I don't care who they are, I'm murdering.* He strolled outside of his home, a warm smile on his face.

He had put on a brown trench coat before leaving, as it was chilly outside. He could shut that out of his mind of course. His mind was meticulously trained. It would be seen as strange to be walking around in this weather without a coat though.

He walked for a little while and did not see anyone, but it was the middle of the night so it was not surprising in Augusta, the town that always sleeps. He kept walking and walking and then he saw headlights approaching on the road. *That's good enough,* he thought, and pointed at the car with his palm upraised and pinky and ring finger folded in.

The driver slammed on the gas and took off as fast as they could and then swerved to hit a telephone pole. The pole snapped in half and fell on top of the car. He walked over to it.

The pole was lying straight down the middle of the car. The windshield was smashed and the top of the car was all dented in. The driver was a woman in her thirties and had dirty blonde hair. Blonde hair that was now even dirtier, matted with blood. Her head had been saved by the airbag, but the telephone pole had smashed her right shoulder, pulverizing the bone.

The strangler walked up to the car. The driver's side window was still intact. He made a fist with his mind and smashed the glass. The sound was a symphony to his ears as the shards sprayed across the pavement, glittering like Christmas lights. He walked up to the door of the car and put his hands on either side and stared in at the bleeding, confused woman.

He began to speak the certain secret words that would enable him to trap her spirit as his slave. She was in shock and did not seem to be aware of what was going on. Once his incantation was spoken he grabbed her head with his mind and pinned it back against the dashboard. He next forced a large chunk of glass from the windshield through her throat. He could feel her life fade fast and that sudden erotic rush of power flowed into him.

It was a beautiful feeling and it invigorated him and he hadn't even had to lift a finger. A smile lit up his face, making him look almost handsome, and he began to walk away before anyone could show up, and even if they did they would think it was a horrible and gruesome car accident. While tragic, there was nothing criminal about it.

He did not head home, though. He decided to continue on his constitutional. It was late at night, though, so there just weren't enough people out and about. The lack of victims was starting to put him in a bad mood. *I'm not gonna let it get to me, more must die.* It's time that people wake up a little to the evil that is lurking beneath the surface of this quiet town. Sure, he had killed plenty before, but now it was time to kick it up a notch.

He walked about a mile away and down several streets from the accident when he spotted his charnel house. He smiled. The house was glowing a bright red and he knew that meant that there was unfinished business in that house. All the lights were out but two cars were in the garage.

He walked up to the door and thought of the key. The door unlocked itself for him. He smiled. When you're doing what you are meant to do everything's so easy. He floated a couple of inches through the door, speaking the old charm again. He folded his legs up and continued levitating inside the house. His feet would not touch the floor the entire time he was there. He made an ax in his mind and in a moment he was holding the black hideous thing. He wanted to feel it.

It was a wicked instrument, all jagged and deadly. The whole thing from handle to blade was blacker than black. It looked as if it was made of one piece of alien metal. He expanded his mind to fill the house. Four people, he could feel them. They were all sleeping. It was a family: man, wife, son, and daughter. He floated up the stairs to the parents' bedroom. *Chop chop* he thought and snickered.

He opened the door to their room and floated in. He sealed it with his mind so that the sound would not wake the young ones. He slammed the bedroom door, but only let it wake the parents. Both of the happy sleepers woke in a most unpleasant manner.

"Someone better be dead," the man in the bed grumbled, sitting up in the dark and switching on the bedside lamp.

"Someone will be dead," Franklin said, cackling and raising his horrible instrument in a most intimidating fashion. He couldn't resist having a little bit of fun and wasn't above a certain amount of drama now and then. The woman screamed sweet music into his ears and his heart rejoiced. The man fumbled for what must be a gun in the night table. Franklin laughed even more insanely at this pitiful attempt, intoxicated by their fear. He swung the ax down severing both of the man's hands in one ghastly blow. The clock radio by the bed suddenly turned on and "Ramblin' Man" by Hank Williams came on. The strangler paused for a second to interpret the old country sounds.

It was the man's turn to scream now and the woman jumped out of the bed, pissing herself. The scent of urine began to overpower the scent of fear as it rushed out of her and though the nightgown onto the bed and floor and her legs. She did not seem to notice it though, preoccupied with blubbering in the corner. Franklin thought she might be praying but it was too incoherent for him to be sure.

He finished the handless man, opening his chest wide open with another swing of the huge ethereal ax. The man was quieter now, just the earthy sound of him shaking out the rest of his life. Franklin turned to look at the woman in the corner.

She would be beautiful if she wasn't covered with piss and snot, he thought, and he wondered if he should have his way with her for a moment.

"You've never been lovelier my dear," he said to be chivalrous, but it wasn't true and he wasn't in the mood for love now.

Instead, he swung the ax around and up, striking her between the legs with the long black blade. He had pushed on the ax with his mind as well as his arms and it went a good four inches into her pelvis. The music was really blasting now. Only with his supernatural strength was he able to free the ax from her flesh, and his next swing was a diagonal slash across the length of her face. He just grazed her, not wanting her dead quite yet and the ax had split her face open from her chin all the way up until it sliced one of her eyes in half. She slumped back onto the ground, one hand trying to hold her face together through the gushing blood and the other trying to hold her guts in. She wasn't long for this world.

Franklin picked her up with his mind slamming her off the ceiling and flattening her out on the floor. He laughed again. That should give the cops something to think about. He held her down on the floor in a superman like pose but face up. He raised the ax high touching the roof with the tip of the blade. He had made the terrible ax blade longer than the wife was wide and it slammed down cutting her completely in

183

half. He flung her halves in opposite directions and the blood and gore flowed free, and the smell of urine and fear were overshadowed by the horrible scent of death and internal gases.

"Let the world know that I have come," Franklin cried, his arms flailing in secret patterns causing his seal to be left in three foot diameter on the wall above the bed in the cow's blood.

This room was done but he was only halfway finished in the night's work so next he went to the son's room down the hall. He felt supercharged more than was normal even with the three murders he had just committed. He knew then that something terrible had happened at this house once and it was a haunted place. He could tell it was both feeding off of and feeding him, and it was as hungry for blood as he was. What an interesting place this 667 Riverside Drive was.

He was not the sort of man to let a haunted house down, so he barged into the son's room. He looked about five and was sleeping in a bed shaped like a race car. That's cute he thought as he willed the kid to rise from the bed and held him upside down over the mattress by a couple of feet.

This woke the kid up and he started screaming a high pitched girlish scream that was not destined to escape the room.

"Shut it!" Franklin said, and swung the ax, decapitating the boy in the blue footie pajamas. The small severed head he let fly off and land on a beanie chair. He continued his hold on the body and allowed all the blood to gush out, soaking the bed and floor of the room. The body next began spinning at his command spraying blood all over him and the walls of the room. Next he let it drop onto the floor and roll under the bed. There was a certain sense of artistry in arranging these scenes for the police.

He had left the daughter for last, as she was meant for more he could sense. She was fourteen and he had something extra special in line for her. He had to be fast because he had dreamed of this before and knew this would be the night he met his prophet. The prophet would be coming by to see him, drawn to the slaughter like a moth to a burning monk.

Chapter 17
Daddy's Home

It had been fun having the house for just her and Millie, but Trish was glad her parents were coming back today. She missed them and felt safer with them around. She just knew great things were going to happen today. She had woken up to the exciting news that the Sand Hill Side Strangler had struck again in his most over the top performance yet.

Triple homicide (what showmanship!) with a possible fourth victim missing, she thought, drinking her morning cup of coffee. Her eyes had been glued to the screen all morning and her panties damp. She was supposed to be in school right now, but with the new murder and her parents coming home today, she had decided to stay home and get stoned watching the news.

She also figured she'd do some house cleaning, to keep the parental units happy. She didn't mind doing chores. Cleaning wasn't too bad when you're high off your ass.

She was knocked out of her reverie when the phone's cacophonous ring cut through the air like a buzz saw. The fear swept over her body as she decided to let the machine get it. It's probably the school. The machine beeped and she could hear Millie. She picked up the phone.

"Hey, Millie. Sorry I didn't make it today. I over slept."

"Yeah . . . I noticed. Can't say as I blame you, bitch. Can you still get me after school? Oh my fuck, did you hear about the latest murders?"

"Yeah, I'm watching it on the news now. I'll be there at two. Mom and daddy will be back today too."

"You think I could forget something like that?"

"Oh yeah. I'll see you at two, dollface, kiss, kiss."

"All right, lazy bones. Love ya."

Trish hung up the phone and sat back down on the couch. She looked across to the large stack of dirty dishes piled up and sighed. Oh well, I guess I better get started on those. I think I need some motivation. She went into her bedroom and opened her stash box. She crushed up a couple of Adderall pills and snorted them.

She could feel the speedy kick right away and she went to work in a flurry around the house. She managed to get everything done by one, giving her a half hour to "relax" before she had to drive into town and pick up Millie.

It was a pleasant drive, and she cranked up Acid Bath loud on the car stereo. She sang along with the beautiful melodies rising over the slow and heavy Louisiana sludge.

She met Millie at the sandwich shop around the corner from school as was their custom on days Trish skipped. Millie was walking out the door as she pulled up holding two 16 ounce energy drinks in her hands.

"You are the best, Millie!" Trish said as she got in and handed one over. She cracked the top on it and guzzled the sweet liquid happiness.

"I know how to treat a girl," Millie said, and they started driving back.

"They are saying there were extreme mutilations in these recent killings on the news. They think he might be losing it and self-destructing," Trish said.

"Sounds like psycho-babble crap to me. Those assholes are so worried about their jobs they'd say anything to make it seem like it was almost over. But it was a real gutsy thing to do. Sandy's kicking into overtime, it would seem. We'll probably see more bullshit tabloid werewolf type articles in the paper to distract the people, I bet," Millie said.

"I know, it's like how stupid do they think that we are? I mean, like, who's even gonna believe that shit?"

"That's so true. I mean, I might believe in some pretty weird shit, you know, but you have to have a cut off somewhere, and with me it's werewolves. That's where I'm drawing the line. I mean, as if," Millie said.

"Totally. Knock on wood, though, just in case," Trish added, laughing.

"I know. As soon as I said that I was picturing a werewolf popping up in the back seat. Those absolute statements can be a biiiiiitch!"

The time was passing slow again as the girls returned to the house and awaited the return of Trish's biological and Millie's de facto parents. Millie loved the Ackermans far more than she loved her birth parents and was always a little bit jealous of Trish for being born into it, but all the Ackermans welcomed her in like she was one of their own.

It had just felt right from the beginning, as soon as she started hanging out with Trish when they were eleven. She could tell they were different right away from all the other people she had ever met before. She remembered waking up one night at a sleepover a few months into their friendship.

They had been sleeping in the same bed together in their cute little nighties. She lay there waiting for Trish to come back to bed, thinking she must be in the bathroom, but she didn't come back.

Little Millie had gotten out of bed and was very surprised by what she had seen. She walked out into the living room and there was Trish and her mom on the couch. Trish's mom, Rachelle, was sitting on the couch in a silken robe. Her long brown hair framed her thin face. She had the robe parted and her bare breast was exposed.

Millie could only see a small part of the breast, however, because Trish was firmly latched onto it, sucking away. Rachelle was stroking Trish's hair and cooing to her. Trish's legs were curled up on the couch next to her mother. Rachelle looked up and saw Millie and smiled.

Millie remembered being scared she'd be in trouble, but Rachelle called her over and said it was OK. She opened the other side of her robe, baring her other boob to Millie. For a second Millie didn't know what to do, but Trish looked so happy.

Millie took the nipple in her mouth and sucked it. Her mouth was filled with the tiniest spray of sweet, warm milk. It was the sweetest and best tasting thing she could remember. She closed her eyes and sucked and sucked that delicious nectar. Rachelle stroked her hair and they nursed like twin sisters together on the couch before going back to bed.

She knew that was a special thing and she never told anyone else about it. She never considered it a sexual thing because it wasn't. Trish had later told her that the longer you breast fed the closer it bonded you and gave you a higher IQ. Trish's mom was out of the school of parenting that let the child decide when she was ready to stop.

So Millie really did feel like a daughter to Rachelle and Vincent Ackerman, especially after that.

"What are you thinking about, dopey?" Trish cut in.

"Chemicals, killers, and chaos," Millie said with an enigmatic smile.

"Well, I think they are here at last," Trish said, rising off the couch to peer out the window.

She could see her parents' black van pulling into the driveway. The girls raced outside to meet them. Vincent Ackerman got out, smiling at his pretty girls running up to meet him. He hugged them both as his wife Rachelle exited the other side of the van. The girls hugged her and helped carry in the bags from the trip.

"How did everything go, pumpkin?" Vincent asked.

"Pretty good, daddy. We did both stores just like you asked, no problem."

"I heard all about it. You're a woman now. Congratulations, sweetie. Don't worry, though, I can always protect my girls."

"We had to kill that guy. He came at me, and I warned him," Trish said, starting to pout.

"I know, sweetie, don't worry about it. I wouldn't risk you getting in trouble, you should know that. The guy working there was one of ours, if you didn't notice. He fed a bullshit story to the cops and I know they bought it."

"How do you know that, daddy?"

"The particulars you do not need to know, pumpkin. Where's Frank? I want to meet him ASAP."

"I haven't talked to him yet today. He said someone might be after him yesterday. I helped him get a gun."

"He needed a gun, huh? Let's hope it kept him safe, for all our sakes. Millie, try and call him now, we need that kid alive."

Millie picked up the portable phone and dialed the number but only the machine picked up. She left a message asking him to call as soon as he got the message, no matter what time it was. Vincent left, saying he had to grab some more things from the van.

He got in the van and drove it into the garage and parked it. Once inside, he had the garage door closed, He opened the back doors and unloaded several crates. He placed these in an empty giant blue freezer. He padlocked it shut and returned to the house.

"How was your trip, daddy?" Trish asked.

"It was good, sugar plum. Daddy got some new supplies that are going to be a lifesaver, I suspect."

He laughed at that.

"Is it firearms? Did you get firearms? Oh please tell me," Trish begged.

"Yes, sweetie, I got quite an arsenal, but you're going to have to wait to see them."

"We missed you guys so much, daddy!" Trish said and pouted.

"We really did," Millie said, putting her sad face on too and putting her arm around Trish's shoulders so they looked like two sad sacks.

"Oh, don't give me those mule lips girls. I have presents for you two." The girls laughed and shrieked and jumped up and down.

"You girls play your daddy something fierce," Rachelle said, swatting Trish lightly on the bottom.

"You know he loves it," Trish said.

"Close your eyes, both of you close 'em, and stick out your hands."

They did as instructed.

"No peeking!" he said, and there was more giggling. Vincent reached into his jacket pocket and placed a hand grenade in each girl's hand.

The girls screamed and leapt for joy, wrapping their arms around the tall, muscular man.

"Easy, now, girls, you'll blow us all up, and we are meant for bigger and better things."

"Oh, Vinny, do you really think the girls at their age need hand grenades? You already gave them guns. When is it going to end? Are you going to give them a flame thrower next? Will they be safe enough then, Vinny?" Rachelle said in a mock exasperated tone.

"A young girl in today's society needs to protect herself from the perils and pitfalls that abound. What if the Strangler went for one of them? Why, you wouldn't want our daughter to shoot the strangler would you? Now with a hand grenade she could fend him off. You gotta think logically woman. Now go and get me a bourbon."

Rachelle shook her head and sighed and went to get the drink. Sometimes there was just no reasoning with men.

The peaceful calm of the household was once again shattered by the ringing of the phone. Millie was closest to it and answered.

"Ackerman residence, Millie speaking," Mildred said.

"Put Vincent on sweetheart," a gruff voice said.

"One moment, please." She handed the phone to Vincent.

"Yeah," Vincent said into the receiver.

"Someone's offering us a deal you need to hear about."

"How soon?"

"Right now."

"Come over."

"I can be there in fifteen." Vincent hung up the phone.

"Make a whiskey sour too, darling. Ron's stopping by," Vincent called over to his wife, who was at the bar in his living room. He loved that bar, it had a record player built into it—very classy. He was curious about this deal. He couldn't imagine what anyone would have to offer them.

"Girls, you are going to have to go up to your room for a little while." They knew better than to argue and each gave him a kiss on the cheek and went upstairs. Rachelle put on a Sinatra record and made herself a martini. Vincent walked over and took a sip of his drink. He hated waiting. It always made him think of his time on the moon.

Rachelle picked up an old faded leather drawstring pouch off the top of the bar and shook it vigorously before spilling its contents onto the bar top. The old bones tumbled out and Rachelle studied the pattern.

"What do them bones say, darling?" Vincent asked, slapping her on her still firm ass. She was 36 but didn't look a day over 25. She never failed to turn him on in their nineteen year marriage.

"These bones are crazy. Something of great spiritual significance is about to happen. It could be trouble. There is a lot of danger around us." Vincent thought he could have come up with that but he kept it to himself. He knew the bones were right though. Damn it, I wish Ron would get here. Not even the Sinatra and the 1792 were soothing his nerves. He put on his smoking jacket and lit a Cuban cigar.

"Roll those bones again, baby," Vincent said.

Rachelle scooped them up and dropped them back in the bag. She shook it up and dumped it again. This time the bones spilled out in the shape of a perfect cross.

"Well, that's peculiar and unsettling," he said, and she just shrugged.

He could hear the girls blasting some sort of heavy music with fast electronic drums carrying through the ceiling, giving Sinatra's crooning a really moving rhythm section and producing a surreal effect.

"I like this new Sinatra remix," Vincent said, dancing around the room to amuse his wife. She cracked up.

"Do you need me for anything, honey? I want to jump in the shower," she asked.

"No, dear, I have everything under control."

She walked out of the living room into the kitchen and up the stairs.

Vincent sat in his easy chair with his feet up until Ron arrived. He heard the car pull into the driveway and rose to meet Ron at the door. Ron was not a man to waste time on pleasantries.

"Someone says they know who he is, and they will tell for two million."

"They know who the fucking strangler is?" Vincent asked, his eyes wide with shock. They had been searching for him over two years.

"Yeah, I think they do and they want to sell it to us."

"We'll pay, no problem. Who is it?"

"Jack Valenti."

"The mobster? Why's he coming to us? And why does he only want two million do you think?"

"Well, Vincent, I think he's trying to be practical instead of greedy. Everyone's looking for this guy. The government wants to cut him up, the mob wants to sell him to the highest bidder on the international market. Valenti just happened to be the guy who found him first, and he's smart. He knows with everyone else the end for him is certain death. He just wants enough money to escape from it all, take his fucking boyfriend to a tropical island and drink fruity umbrella drinks or something."

"I should be able to get a check cut tomorrow. Where is this guy? I want him brought in."

"I'm not sure where he is right now. He hasn't been answering the phone."

"I want him found, and not let out of our sight until he has told us who the Strangler is. Holy shit, this is an amazing blessing. We cannot screw this up. This is our chance. Use everything and everyone we have at our disposal."

Chapter 18
Killing time

Frank hated waiting too and this was the worst kind. He was not feeling great as he sat there in the half light of various electronics, clutching a handgun and waiting for his man. He had sent Josette out to the road to watch for Valenti. The creepy clown painting was really starting to get to him. The thing was like a magic eye Jesus and wherever he went he could feel its eye on him. While the subject matter may not have been quite as disturbing as in the Bosch pieces he had seen earlier, it was still bizarre and somehow much more unsettling.

The painting was larger than life size, unless this clown was eight feet tall. The painting was full length and the bottom of it where the giant red clown shoes were shown was only a couple of inches off the floor. The clown was modeling its tubby clown body in what was clearly a sexual manner. He had one white clown gloved hand behind his head, and the other one was on his hip. Frank began thinking of him as Scary the Clown. Scary's grease painted mug was split open and a very long tongue was protruding in a rude leer. Scary also featured the most frightening eyes he had ever seen on a painting. It did not please him. It did not please him at all.

The gun in his hand was looking less and less powerful. Fuck it, I got a ghost keeping watch, I might as well search the place. I must be able to find something stronger than this pea shooter in this criminal's den.

Frank was correct and found a shotgun and some shells in the closet in the bedroom. That's more like it, he thought and grabbed the gun. It was fully loaded, of course. He put his handgun back into his pants.

Walking back into the living room Frank had to fight the urge to shoot the giant wicked clown. He set down the shotgun and walked over to the painting and took it off the wall. He turned the giant thing around and leaned it against the wall. He knew that the hideous thing was still on the other side but at least he wouldn't give it the pleasure of eye fucking him any longer.

The clown issue dealt with, he began to get hungry. This lead to rifling through the refrigerator. Another surprise it was fully stocked with excellent and fancy food.

Valenti must have a girlfriend that is a chef or something, he realized, and started to worry a little that the wrong person might come home. Frank had a hard time picturing mobster Jack Valenti buying avocados, hummus, and feta cheese. Someone else must either live here or spend a lot of time here. He decided to check the bedroom for a woman's clothing after making a monstrous sandwich.

He put Cajun turkey and Swiss cheese on rye with garlic Mayo, avocado slices, tomato, and onion. He wolfed it down fast and he enjoyed it. It was satisfying in some primal way to eat his victim-to-be's food.

If Valenti's girlfriend or anyone else showed up, he'd have to kill them. It was his only choice now. That could really screw everything up though. If he blew Valenti's girl away with a shot gun he'd have to get the hell out of here, and he'd still have Valenti to deal with. A much more angry and ready Valenti. That was definitely not what he wanted. He needed that element of surprise.

He did not find any women's clothing in the bedroom, just some lube. He wasn't sure what to think, and it looked like his time was about up. He went through the drawers in the desk and found some pictures.

"Holy shit," Frank said out loud. There was an identical Polaroid of Jack Valenti among the pictures as the one that had been left for him in the graveyard. Frank folded the picture and slipped it into his back pocket. He looked up. Josette was floating toward him.

"It is almost time, Frank, are you ready to kill?"

"Yes, dear."

Josette said, "Get down on your knees, Frank."

He did as she asked and she floated in front of him. She bent down and kissed his cheek, but he did not feel a thing. She looked into his eyes and pressed one finger to her lips, letting him know to be quiet. He nodded.

She lifted her arms up and began chanting in a long-dead language. Frank could hear the blood rushing in his head. He almost collapsed. He was seeing these flashes, bits and pieces of scenes. They were telling a story, but it was too fast and he could not put it together. The room flashed red then blue, and she stopped chanting abruptly and reached and rubbed Frank's head. It felt wet. He couldn't feel her hand, but he could feel the wet stuff she rubbed on it.

"You are ready now, Frankie," the ghost said. "So it is done."

"So it is done."

The spectral little girl flew away from him through the wall then ducked in again.

"There's a car pulling into the driveway, Frank," she said.

"Go see if it's a man or a woman," he said. Maybe if it was the girlfriend he could just run out of the hole in the sliding glass doors and come back another time. He needed to do this right. The front door of the house opened up and then the entryway went up six steps to reach the living room. Frank was laying down at the top of the stairs pointing the shotgun at the door. He had the pistol laying on the floor next to him.

"It's the man from the photo," Josette called.

Frank concentrated all his attention on the brass door handle waiting for it to wiggle. Your ass is mine, Valenti. Then he heard it, the slight sound of the key snapping into the lock. Frank let Valenti get the door unlocked, but didn't wait for him to open it. He aimed for the center of the door and pulled the trigger.

One second later he was deaf. It was the loudest thing he had ever heard before he could even feel the kick of it slam into his shoulder. He tried to shake the confusion out of his head. He set down the shotgun and grabbed the handgun. He leapt from the top of the stairs, and opened what was left of the buckshot shredded door.

Valenti was lying on his back, blood everywhere, but he was not dead. The tough bastard was trying to get a gun out of his ankle holster. Frank pulled his gun up and fired again. He could not have been more than seven feet from Valenti, but somehow, cold hearted killer though he was determined to be, he missed. Jack rolled to the side with a groan and managed to get his gun free. Frank heard three cannon shots in a row and the next thing he knew he was on the ground and blood was spraying out of him. He could not feel any pain yet and he looked around and saw his gun on the ground next to him. He grabbed it as the pain washed over him.

"I've been waiting to pay you back you, motherfucker!" Valenti shrieked and put a lead reminder in Frank's gut. Frank grimaced and fired a burst of three shots that caught Valenti in the neck and face. Valenti's corpse pitched backward head over heels from Frank.

Strength surged into him and Frank stood up the proud victor. He could feel himself growing stronger, he was starting to feel a little bit of pain but only a pleasant tickle. He let out a primal roar and his mouth was filled with blood. Hot delicious blood. He passed out.

He woke up feeling fine. He was covered in blood, both his and Valenti's. He ran his hand across his chest but the skin was unbroken and perfect under the bullet holed shirt. The pain and wounds were completely gone. He picked up Valenti's body and was surprised by how light it felt. He brought the body into the house and hung it upside down.

He sent Josette out to watch the street for cops or anyone else. After no one showed up in fifteen minutes he figured he was safe and called Spider.

"Yeah," Spider answered.

"I'm all finished here. Care to go on a treasure hunt? There's gotta be some good stuff here. I'm pretty sure the coast is clear," Frank said.

"That sounds excellent. I'll be right over," Spider said and hung up the phone.

He wasn't kidding either. Somehow he made it in five minutes. Frank had time to go into the bathroom and look in the mirror.

"Whoa," he said out loud. It was quite mind blowing. He lifted his bloody shirt and the bullet holes were completely gone. He was amazed.

Spider just parked in the driveway this time. He made his way into the house through the shambles of the door.

"Mind the blood," Frank called.

"It's all right, I didn't like this pair of shoes anyway. Mind turning on a fucking light," Spider said.

Frank hadn't even noticed the lights were all off and he could see everything. He flipped on a switch for Spider's benefit. He stared at the hung upside down dead body and laughed.

"And you said I was a complex person," Spider commented, approving the grim scene.

"I only searched a little bit and found this shotgun but there's gotta be some treasure around here somewhere I figure. You've been so helpful I thought we could split anything we find here."

"That works for me. I bet there is some money around here somewhere, I can smell it," Spider said, and began looking around the place; looking for places where he might put something if he lived there. Frank went to the bedroom and started looking through the drawers.

Nothing in there but men's clothes, but he noticed there was a briefcase under the bed. It had a lock on it, but he carried it into the kitchen and pried it open with a knife.

"Holy motherfucking shit!" Frank yelled as he opened the briefcase and tried to take inventory of the contents.

"What did you find?" Spider said, walking into the room.

"Only Hunter Thompson's brief case from the looks of it! Look at this gigantic stash! There's a quarter pound of sweet green, what looks like an ounce of coke, fifty pills of ecstasy, straight DXM, LSD, special K and even some fuckin' DMT."

"Wow, are you sure?" Spider said. He looked into the brief case and laughed. Everything was clearly labeled.

I'm alive and I now have a suitcase full of drugs—this is the best day ever!

"Hail Satan!" Frank exclaimed, moved by the moment. Spider went back to looking around and found a hidden opening in the wall where guns and cash were stashed. There were five antique revolvers and ten grand in cash.

"How about this Spider, I take 5 large, and the drugs and you get the other 5 and the guns and electronics if you want 'em."

"Okay, but I get the shotgun too."

"Of course."

They loaded Spider's car up and got the fuck out.

Chapter 19
Payback

"What do you want to do today, brother?" Tess asked.

"I don't care. Whatever you want to do is fine," Josh said. He wasn't really paying attention as he was watching the news. They were busy talking about his new friend.

"Hey, I know that guy," Josh said.

"You know Robert Murphy, star reporter?"

"No, I know the killer. I met him when I went out last night."

"No way. You're full of shit!" Tess exclaimed. She lit a big joint and took a massive hit into her tiny lungs.

"It's true! He cast some sort of spell on me so I had to obey him. Other than that he seemed like a nice enough guy."

"That's a pretty strange story, brother."

"It's a pretty strange world."

They sat there watching TV and smoking. When the joint was finished, Josh wandered off to his bedroom. It wasn't long before Tess would follow him in there. Josh sat on his bed making a list. Tess walked into his bedroom without knocking.

"Whatcha doing, brother?" she asked.

"I'm making a list."

"What kind of list?"

"I'm making a list of everyone who has done me wrong."

"Oh, a shit list. I like that song."

"That song sucks."

"So what are you going to do with them?"

"I'm gonna fucking eat them, of course. What's the point of being special if you can't get a little payback. Now that's a good song."

"You're so lucky, brother. I'm so jealous. Oh, let me put a couple people on the list please, please."

"Yeah, all right, but quit your whining it's annoying." Then he added in his best James Brown impersonation (which sounded more like Louis Armstrong), "That's it, payback! Revenge . . . I'm mad!"

"Who's on the top of your list? We already ate mom and dad?" Tess asked.

"Mrs Apricotface. Oh, that bitch is gonna get it now. Throw me out of her class. Well, guess who's a fucking werewolf now?"

"You, you!" Tess shouted.

"That was a rhetorical question little sis."

"I don't care what kind it was, I got it right!"

"If they only had an aptitude test for werewolf, they might have known better than to mess with me. Stupid idiots. It's too late for assholes though. Everyone on this grocery list is gonna end up ground chuck. So who do you want to add?"

"Mary Lou! She's been so mean to me for so long. She said the most horrible things about our family. You should really make her suffer. You should rape her."

"But that might turn her into a werewolf."

"Well, then, you are just going to have to rip her in half before that happens."

"Oh, right. Screw you, Mary Lou."

"That's the spirit. Oh, I want to be there. She has to know it's because of me. She needs to know that or it doesn't mean a damn thing."

"I could always tell her, you know. Be like . . . look, this one's for my sister, Tess. You mess with her, you're messing with me. Now get ready for a serious raping!"

"Don't take the look on her face away from me, brother. I couldn't stand to miss it. That special moment when she realizes she's gonna get raped to death by a werewolf because of me." Tess jumped up and down and clapped.

"Yeah, okay, sick-o, you can ride shotgun on that one since it means so much to you. I'd hate to stand in the way of your delinquency and perversion, you know. But you're gonna have to postpone your ecstasy, for a little while at least, because it's Mrs Apricotface that's on the top of this shit list and I done checked it twice."

"You gonna fuck her too?"

"Yeah, right, maybe with a chainsaw I could penetrate those beef curtains."

"Brother, you don't have a chainsaw!"

"The hell I don't."

"Do you really think you need a chainsaw. I mean, come on, you're a fucking werewolf, bro."

"I know I don't need one, but it's still fun to accessorize. Werewolves are scary, I'll give you that, but a werewolf with a chainsaw . . . I mean, you see one of those and you're really gonna shit your fucking pants. That's terrifying. Here's this giant primal monster wolf that wants to kill you and look, he's even learned how to use tools to kill you even fucking deader. That's me, baby. A werewolf of the two thousands."

"Hey, I ain't a baby."

"Wah, wah."

"Brother, I'm not a baby. I'm plenty old!"

"Cool your jets, you're my baby sister, that's all I mean. Now go get me the fucking phone book."

Tess knew better then to press her luck and went and got it. She handed it to Josh and he began flipping through it.

"So you're a werewolf of the two thousands teamed up with the last century's tree cutting technology."

"Hey, there's a techno curve for werewolves. We're beasts. Maybe in another fifty years there will be werewolves with lasers, or maybe a werewolf on the moon. That'd be pretty cool."

"That would be pretty cool. I can just see him now, with a space helmet on," Tess said. The conversation switched gears as Josh found what he wanted.

"Eugenia Apricotface, there she is! It even gives the address and everything, Tess. Man, how did this bitch ever live this long, you know what I mean?"

"I wanna go, I wanna go!" Tess shrieked.

"This ain't no carnival. You sure you're ready to ride this ride? It's gonna get pretty gory."

"Showers of gore, showers of blood," Tess sang, feeling happy.

"You sound ready to me. Let's go get it on." He motioned for her to follow him. He took the family car and began driving over to Mrs Apricotface's house, though he had not even a drivers permit!

"Are you sure it's a good idea to drive over there? What if someone sees the car? We don't want people at the house asking all sorts of questions."

"No, we don't. I'm going to park it a couple blocks over. Then we'll hoof it. You want to have some fun?"

"I love fun. Fun's my middle name."

"Then how about you go up to the house and get her to let you in."

"How would I do that? It's the middle of the night."

"I don't know, Tess, be creative. You're always saying you want to be a movie star, so act. Make up a story."

Tess was silent. Josh could almost see the smoke rising from her sweet little head.

"I guess I could say there had been a car accident, and I needed to use the phone."

"That's a classic. Coming from you it will probably work. Maybe try to cry some."

"Okay, I'll just have to try to think of something sad. Hmmm. Does Mrs Apricotface have a husband?"

"That dried up old bag? Not likely."

"So funny to think her last moments will be spent with me."

"Her second to last, at least. I think she might be focusing a little more on me during her final moments."

"That's fine with me. It's your show, brother."

"I got a surprise in the trunk."

"No way! Is it for me?"

"No, it's not for you. Be quiet now. I just turned on to Mocking Bird Lane. We need to find her house. It's 1314. It should be on your side," Josh said as they proceeded slowly down the dark street. His eyes caught 1313 on a mail box.

"There it is, it's that one across the street from the funeral home," Josh said, pointing it out for his sister.

"I see it." He did not stop but kept driving, took his next left. He drove another block and took another turn and parked.

"Come on, it's show time," Josh said, locking the doors of the car.

"Born on a green light, brother-o."

"Check this out. I wasn't just kidding around. I'm fucking serious."

Josh turned the key and opened the trunk. Tess looked in but all she could see was a blue blanket.

"I don't get it," Tess said.

Josh peeled back the blanket and Tess understood. It was a chainsaw.

Chapter 20
Collusion

Fritz had the best job in the world and he knew it. His current assignment was to kill people and he had really been enjoying himself. He had killed lots of people in his life both in professional and personal capacities. It was his calling, so to speak. Just like how Babe Ruth was meant to hit a ball with a stick, Fritz was a bringer of death.

The US government had realized this and had been following him since high school. They pulled him out of college and gave him a job. Since they had failed to be able to stop people from serial killing, they had stumbled onto a plan to use serial killers in a productive manner.

It didn't work with all of them, but if they fit a certain personality profile, it turned out to be a very beneficial arrangement for both parties. They did as they were told and were protected. License to kill, and dental benefits. You couldn't really ask for more than that, if one was so inclined.

It really was a match made in heaven as the jobs assigned were very pleasurable to that type. This latest one was very strange but fulfilling as well. He had never strangled anyone before and there was something very romantic and erotic about it. It made Fritz feel like a real lover of women.

He knew they were keeping him in the dark about some kind of sensitive information. They weren't sure how some of the original victims had been killed. He didn't care though, he wasn't afraid. He was tough and he doubted that he himself was in much danger. He was wrong though, and just about to find out how much.

Today was the day he would find the imposter, he was confident. He felt that yesterday's splurge would lure the imposter out in the open. Then he would squash him like a bug, before he screwed things up anymore, or made things easier for the authorities to cover everything that had happened up.

He didn't plan on doing the cops any favors. Lucky for him, tonight was ladies night and his dear wife was playing bridge with the girls. He went out to the garage and lit some incense. He sat in the lotus position and began meditating.

He rose from his sitting body and floated out like a ghost through the closed garage door. He rose into the night sky and searched for the imposter. It was not for any practical reason that the strangler searched but it was a part of the ritual that had been played out over and over again ad nauseam. The end was not the destruction of the imposter himself, but the ritual defense of his position.

There was a lot of evil lurking under the surface in Augusta, and he knew he was approaching this problem from the wrong angle. He decided to try something new. He returned to his body, but stayed in the trance. He began to imagine himself expanding. He felt himself expanding until he was aware of the whole garage and everything within it. There were thousands of things in the garage and suddenly his mind raced with newfound rush of everything and its exact location. It was an amazing feeling, and this was not an area he had ventured in before.

He continued to stretch himself out but he was not able to go much further while absorbing everything so he had to loosen up, and he let go of the knowledge of objects and just focused on people. That opened it up for him and he raced out in all directions at once, scouring the city.

He was scanning through all the people, boring men and woman for the most part. Five miles away he found his man. He was in the basement cleaning out a cell. He was intending to go out and get a girl. He was cleaning up after the last one that had been there.

His real name was Fritz Herring, and he worked for the FBI. He lived in this house under a fake name. Franklin learned this and everything else about this man instantly as he focused his full attention on him. After scanning him he dove into the man's body and took control.

Possession was not an easy thing to achieve for the living but Franklin as a master of the temple could do it. He grabbed Fritz and put him in a little cage in the back of his mind. Franklin was very happy and his happiness fed him even more strength.

He walked out of the basement and picked up the phone in the kitchen, and called Fritz's boss. He was in a temporary headquarters in a rented house in Augusta with ten other agents and a whole lot of computers.

"Why are you calling me? This isn't one of our scheduled times?"

"I stumbled on some important information you need to hear in person—"

"Are you sure? This is not supposed to really hap—"

"You want to hear this, I kno—"

"DON'T SAY IT! Come on over."

"I'll be right there," Franklin said from Fritz's mouth. He grabbed Fritz's .44 Bulldog and car keys and was out the door. Augusta wasn't that big, and the house was only six miles away.

He walked up to the door and he was let in. Two agents walked him to Ronald Weissenburg, the man he had spoken to on the phone.

He was too quick for them and the .44 came out from its barely concealed position under his coat. Ronald only had time to open his mouth before he was shot in the face. His brains and head fluids splattered the wall behind him in the shape of a pentagram.

Franklin turned and pointed his gun at the other two but they had already drawn their weapons and were shooting him in the chest. He pulled the trigger of the gun, unloading the rest of the rounds into the other two agents.

His body went numb and he realized one of the bullets had pierced his heart and killed him. Fritz was gone. Franklin didn't let go, though, he reloaded. He stomped on the throats of the other agents to make sure they were dead as more swarmed into the room.

He killed another four agents before the body took a head shot and he was blasted back to his own body, where he awoke with a smile on his face and an erection. It felt good to have sent those pompous presumptuous apes a lesson. How dare they interfere with his great work. They didn't understand it and never would. You'd have to be a 33rd degree mason to even guess.

He had a feeling he might not be long for this world. Things were getting exciting. He would have to go out tonight and harness more energy.

He still had a lot to do. It was time to call the wolf. He concentrated. *Come to me, come to me now.* He knew the wolf had heard him. He would be here soon. Franklin walked out into the kitchen.

He put the frozen pizza in the preheated oven. He loved pizza. This kind had cheddar stuffed in the crust which made it extra fulfilling. He went over to the stereo and decided to put in some dinner music. He was feeling dramatic so he chose Carl Orff's "Carmina Burana."

Ah yes, this is an inspiring piece, he thought as he put the kettle on for tea. He had just poured the water into the cup when he heard three knocks on the door. He walked over to the front door and let Josh in.

"Hello. Josh. How are you today?"

"I'm a little busy today, I'm afraid. Is this important?" Josh asked.

Franklin chuckled.

"Yes, it is important, Josh. Would you care for some pizza?" Franklin said.

"Well, you see, I got my little sister in the car and I'm in the middle of chainsaw murdering someone right now, but sure I guess I'll have a slice if it's hot."

"Good choice. Follow me," Franklin said and led him into the kitchen. He opened up the stove and removed the pizza stone. He began slicing the pizza as he continued talking.

"What do you mean you're in the middle of it? Is the prey dead?"

"Well, yeah, but—"

"But nothing, it's done then. They have been murdered successfully, and the good news is you got away. Now don't go back to the scene of the crime. That's elementary! Also, you have something of far greater importance to do. I have a task for you and it must be done now. You're gonna have to leave your sister here. This must be done alone."

"She's just a girl. You're not gonna hurt her are—"

Franklin raised the pizza cutter, silencing Josh.

"Don't worry. I don't want to hurt her. Invite her in so she can have a piece while you run this errand for me."

"Okay, but know this, I love my sister, and only my sister, in this world."

"Come on, now, that's not necessary. I am almost fully illuminated."

Josh went back to the car. Tess was listening to Slayer in the CD player.

"Come on, you've been invited to a pizza party."

"You're shitting me," Tess said, wide eyed.

"No, I'm not, come on. I got something I gotta do, and I gotta do it alone."

"You mean you're fucking leaving me alone with him?"

"I'm afraid so."

"It's cool?"

"It will be," Josh said, and lead her into the house.

"Welcome, Tess. My name is Franklin. Would you care for some pizza and soda?"

"Hello, Franklin. Um, sure."

"I'm sorry to interrupt your evening, but I need your brother for something very important. Enjoy the orange soda It tastes better because it comes from a glass bottle." He passed her over a bottle of soda and a plateful of pizza. "You can go in the living room and watch some television now, dear."

"Thank you," she said and curtsied, then went into the next room.

"Now, Franklin, here is what I need you to do. You know that big old church on the top of my hill?"

"Your hill?" Josh asked.

Franklin just stared at him.

"Oh, yeah. Sand Hill," Josh said.

"You need to destroy it."

"That huge stone one? How am I going to do that? That thing's like a castle made out of tanks."

"You're going to blow it up with plastic explosives."

"Plastic explosives? Wouldn't it be easier for you to just blow it up with magic?"

"The important thing is that you do this. There is no time to explain why that is now, but I can't do this myself. It must be the werewolf. I will give you an address. Go there and in the garage you will find the tools you will need."

"This crust is awesome!" Tess yelled from the other room.

"So why do you wanna blow up this church?" Josh said.

"It's because of the cheddar," Franklin called to Tess before continuing. "Well, Josh, it's not really a church. It's an alien spaceship that's stuck in the ground and we are going to free it. Now get going."

"But I don't even know how to use plastic—"

Franklin cut him off by waving his hand in a slow but smooth arc over Josh's forehead.

"Now you do," Franklin said, and it was true.

"Wow, that's fucking weird, man."

"You had better hurry. It must be done within three hours."

"I had better leave then."

Franklin handed him the address on a folded in half piece of notebook paper.

"I'll drop Tess back off at your house," Franklin said.

"Okay. I'll see you later."

Josh waved goodbye to his sister and walked out the door. He got in the car and looked at the address. It was going to be a long night for this werewolf.

Chapter 21
Sex and Drugs and Stealing Souls

Frank was feeling pretty great. Things seemed to, for once, be going his way. The only problem was there was no one to share it with at this particular moment in time. Spider had dropped him off at his house but no one was home. That was strange as he hadn't heard Dan or Nayte mention any plans, however he had been gone a lot.

He paced back and forth a little and that's when he noticed the flashing light. He walked over to the answering machine and pressed play.

"Hey, Frankie, this is Trish. I was just wondering if you were around! Anyway, my dad is back in town and he really wants to meet you, so give a ring as soon as you get this."

That was a splendid idea, he thought. They were exactly the right people to celebrate with. Frank smiled and he felt his dick get a little bigger at the thought.

He picked up the phone and called Trish's cell. It rang three times before she answered.

"Well, hello stranger," she said.

"Hey, Trish, how's you doing tonight?"

"Better now, I've been trying to get a hold of you all night. We miss you, you know."

"Yeah, I been busy . . . got things to do sometimes . . . you know how that is. Come over here. Is Mildred with you? Pick her up if she ain't. It's fucking party time. No joke. The football is NOT empty!"

"Oooh, sounds nice. Don't worry, lover boy, she's here all right. We'll come and pick you up. You gotta come out here and meet my dad."

"Oh yeah, that sounds awesome . . ."

"Oh, come on, it's not like that."

"Yeah, okay, hurry up then. I got a surprise for you."

"Oh, what is it?"

"I already told you, it's a fucking surprise."

"Oh right. . . what was that again?"

"Smooth. So you gonna be here soon?" Frank said, and gave her directions.

"In a tick, darling."

He hung up and began waiting for the girls to arrive. He figured he probably had a half hour before they would show up. He decided to try out the new ganja. He put the 'Psychedelic sounds of The Thirteenth Floor Elevators' lp in mono on the turn table and cranked that motherfucker up. The sound of that 1966 Texas psychedelic rock smoothed out the wrinkles in his brain.

He got to the business of rolling a joint of the new bright green marijuana from the briefcase. It smelled amazing, like it must have its own funny name. I don't want to be too stoned when the girls arrived he thought and took a look into the briefcase.

Cocaine, that's what I need. He took out the baggie and dumped some out onto a mirror and cut up about ten fat lines, leaving a big pile left on the side of the mirror.

He put the rest of the bag away in the briefcase and took out some LSD, DXM, and Ecstasy.

He measured out 300 milligrams of the dextromethorphan. He did this two more times. Then he called to Josette.

"Hello, Frank!" she called out sweetly.

"Hey, Jo, wanna come to a party?"

"A party? Where?"

"Right here and right now. A couple more guests are on the way."

"Okay, that sounds like fun. You should always rejoice after victory."

"From my heart to your spectral lips, my little ghostie."

"What is that powder you are measuring out?"

"Oh, that? It's only cold medicine. I'm afraid I might be coming down with something."

"Best to avoid that."

"My thoughts as well, little honey."

He heard a car pull in to the driveway and knew it must be them. He could smell them as he focused in and that smell was of sex and youth. A big grin split his face.

They banged on the door and he let them in.

"Hey, girls, come on in, welcome to my party. There's some coke cut up on the mirror over there. Help yourself."

They wrapped their arms around him and he stumbled back, almost falling over at the ferocity of their greeting. He kissed them both open mouthed and they hung on him.

"Good to see you, Frankie," Millie said, and walked over to the mirror and blew a line. Trish was right behind her.

"I think it's about that time for me too," Frank said, and and put one line up each nostril.

"Thanks for the pick me up," Trish said.

"No problem. Sharing is caring."

To illustrate this point he passed the half smoked joint to her. She took it, took two big drags on it, and passed it to Mildred.

"I must say, girls, I used to be kind of depressed sometimes to be honest, but I think I've gotten over it. I may finally be able to understand things as they may be, and it's given me tremendous clarity. For the first time in my life there's actually nothing I can complain about."

"That's great!" Millie said smiling.

"It is. You wanna go for a joy ride with us?" Trish asked.

"I might go for a ride, but it's not going to be that easy. How about we play a fun game? It's sort of like a compromise. I pick out a fun drug cocktail for us to do and then when it kicks in, we can go and do whatever you want."

"Oh, yeah, a drug cocktail, huh? Is that going to be full of hard drugs?" Millie asked.

"You betcha. The hardest."

"I'm in," Millie said.

"Are you sure this is a good idea?" Trish asked. She laughed but she was nervous.

"No!" Millie and Frank chimed in at the same time.

They all laughed and Trish agreed to it.

"All right, then, make us a cocktail bartender!" Millie said.

"But of course, my lady," Frank said, dropping to one knee briefly to kiss her hand.

"First three single ply sheets of toilet paper," he said, and walked into the bathroom that was off the living room by the stairs to the second floor.

"What do you need those for?" Trish asked.

"We are going to parachute this cocktail. You never did that?" he explained while pulling the toilet paper apart until he had the one ply sheets.

"No, what's it mean?"

"It's an easy way to do powders. It gets them to kick in faster. You put the drugs on the paper, fold it up, then swallow it. It breaks down in your stomach and the drugs kick in faster than if your stomach had to break up a pill. It's also a less gross way to take powder orally. First ingredient is 300 milligrams of dextromethorphan. This would be gross as hell if you mixed it in water but you can just swallow it now all at once."

"That's the stuff in cold medicine, right? Wow, you have pure DXM?"

"That's right, I do, and that's not all. Next we are going to add two pills of ecstasy. You wanna give me a hand, Trish?"

She giggled.

"You know, I never mind giving you a hand," she said.

"In the kitchen, go and get two large tablespoons from the silverware drawer."

It took her a couple tries but she soon returned with the requested tools.

"Okay, hold out one spoon." He placed the two pills in the spoon. "Now press them together and be careful not to spill."

The girls were wide eyed at the drugs. When Trish was done he had her dump it out onto one of the toilet paper sheets. They repeated this process until they had the three squares lined up with the DXM and the X.

"Now I'm going to add the LSD," Frank said. It was in an eyedropper bottle and he carefully squeezed out three drops onto each pile.

"Holy shit, I'm not sure if we should get this fucked up. We have to drive out to Windsor later, you know."

"Hey, a deal's a deal. We can always wait off the effects if we have too, or I can drive," Frank said.

"Okay, okay, let's do it," she said.

"It shouldn't be that bad. We're just candy flipping on skis with a robo cushion."

"Let's do it. Right now before I lose my nerve."

He folded up one and popped it in his mouth, washing it down with a swig from a Mountain Dew big slam. He folded up the next one and passed it and the soda to Millie.

"Chug a lug, Millie," he said.

"You only live once, right," she said and tossed it back.

Trish followed without a word.

"Fuck, yeah, now it's on," Frank said.

"Well, what do we do now?" Trish said.

"I'm sure we'll be able to think of something," Frank said and laughed.

"Is that all you ever think of?" Trish asked.

"No, it's not all I think off."

"That's too bad. It's all I think about," she said, dropping to her knees.

"I need a snack. Got anything for me? I'm soooo hungry!"

"Yeah, I think I can find something," Frank said.

He unbuttoned his pants and took out his cock. She put it in her mouth and started drooling. Millie slid her panties down over her boots and spread her legs.

He stared, hypnotized by that smooth patch of loveliness, and did another line. He slid down onto the floor, lying on his back. His cock was buried deep in Trish's hot throat and a moan escaped his lips. Millie was watching Trish suck Frank's cock and true to her compulsive behavior, masturbating like a hurricane.

"Come over here, Millie," he gasped.

She hesitated but walked over across the room on slow tiptoes, then seemed to gain confidence and came and sat on his face. His moaning was muffled by her thighs on either side of his face and she began grinding her clit against his lips. He got really hot but was able to maintain control until the face humping reached a feverish level and she screamed out her orgasm, and the sweet honey dripping into his mouth made him explode. Trish gasped and moaned, trying to gulp down his pulsing seed.

"All right, now this party is started," Frank said, and tried to stand up. He lumbered across the room, arms flailing out, searching for something to grab onto. Somehow he steadied himself, though it felt like he was walking under water.

"That would be old Dex kicking in," he told the girls.

The girls were not fazed and said they couldn't feel anything yet. Frank wasn't too surprised. His system was sensitive to it due to large cycles of prior abuse. But that was a whole different story—one that had brought Frank many different places and had led him to where he was now. It seemed fitting to be dancing with that old devil again tonight.

"You will, trust me, you will. Let's smoke another joint while we wait and see how you feel then."

"Sure, why not."

"You'll probably be tripping your face off by then."

He twisted it up fast while they rocked out to the music. The Elevators were enough to make you feel like you were tripping even if you weren't. Really mind expanding stuff.

They sat there and smoked the joint. Everything was getting brighter and he could feel some of the drugs coming on. He felt this deep chemical joy welling up inside him and it was quite pleasant and frightening.

"You two are the best. I hate to be cheesy, but I just thought you ought to know."

"I feel weird," Trish said.

"Come on into my bedroom. I have something I want to show you," Frank said.

The girls laughed but it was delayed and somehow strange. Things had gotten really trippy.

"Come on, you've already seen that, silly rabbits. That's not what I mean at alllllllll."

He walked through the computer room, leading the way. He got to his room and only Millie was with him.

"Hey, Trish, come on in here," he called out into the living room.

"Sorry, I can't move," she replied from the other room.

"Oh, okay, don't worry about that. That happens sometimes. Just lay there and we'll be back in a moment."

Frank continued into his room with Millie. There were two long shelves attached to the wall. He grabbed an old sketch book off the shelf.

"Check this out. This is freaky. I knew you girls looked familiar, like I had seen you in a dream or something. Well after a while I put my finger on it," he said while flipping through the pictures in the book, and then he found the picture he was looking for.

"Oh, my fucking Devil," Millie said, staring wide eyed at the picture. It was a drawing of two topless girls in Sombreros. They looked just like Millie and Trish, but it was dated a year ago.

"Hey, that looks just like us!" Millie said.

"It gets even weirder. Let's go back in the living room so I don't have to explain twice," Frank said, leading the way once again. They were slowing, lifting their legs up high like they were walking on the moon. He was starting to feel quite fucked up.

"Hey, guys, tell me a story," Trish called, hoarse and on the floor as they sauntered into the room.

"So, Trish, I was just showing Millie this picture I drew a year ago. I was fucked up on cough medicine and drew you two before I even met you." He handed the picture to Trish, who put it right against her face for a close inspection.

"Holy fuck, that flips my grid. Millie, spit in my mouth!" Trish demanded. Millie turned her head and quickly spit into Trish's open mouth.

The phone screams into life and Frank grabs it before its rude song can cut into his ears any further.

"Grand Central Station," he said into the very curvy mouthpiece.

"Hello, Frank, me and Nayte are stranded at the old church on the top of Sand Hill, You think you can come get us?" Dan said.

"Sure, no problem, buddy," Frank said.

"Thanks, man come as soon as you can," Dan said, and hung up.

"We gotta go get Nayte and Dan. They are up on Sand Hill and need a ride," Frank said.

Millie started screaming at the top of her lungs. She was pointing at the corner of the room and hyper-ventilating.

"What is it?" he asked, freaked out by reality's little quirks.

"There's a fucking little girl standing in the corner."

"Oh, fuck me, that's just Josette, nothing to worry about. I didn't think anyone else could see her. You never could before. That's fucking interesting. Real interesting. This phenomena must be documented."

"I can see her too," Trish said with fear in her voice.

"It's not polite to stare," Josette said, and both girls screamed again.

"Hey, now, that's not necessary, I said she was with me," Frank chastised the silly women.

"Sorry . . . little ghost girl . . . dead child friend," Millie said.

"Yeah , we were just surprised," Trish added.

Josette floated closer to the girls.

"It was a surprise to me too. But now we can be friends forever," Josette said, and giggled in her lilting child's soprano.

"Huh, who knows maybe it's the acid, or a side effect from the drug combo. Hmm, it seems like a lucky break maybe . . . or maybe we're all already dead hmmm," Frank said, pondering.

"Well, what do you think we should do now? Should we go to this church, or have we already?"

"I don't know. Someone sure likes to play with pictures, though, I mean, fuckin' A, pictures are following me everywhere, telling me what to do. I'm sick of it. I don't have to take that shit anymore."

"What are you talking about?" Millie asked.

"I'm not sure myself. I got lost there." He sat down on the couch and looked around. He felt like he was in a giant glass Christmas ornament. Everything was bright and rounded at the edges. Light was refracting off everything. Josette was glowing, and Frank felt like he was floating.

The two other girls were beginning to look like cartoon caricatures of themselves, their faces longer and more angular. They looked beautiful as Martians, but he no longer had the attention span for serious sexual arousal.

"How you doing, ladies? I'm pretty messed up. Let's go to church," he said, laughing in their faces until they were scared. He heard the words slow down and speed up, somehow echoing over and over again with flange and distortion and other effects he didn't recognize yet.

"I love you, Frankie," Millie said.

"I love you too, Frank, and you, Millie. I love you. You're like my best friend in the whole wide world."

"Oh, I love you too, Trish. We're like sisters."

"That's the X. Sometimes it makes you talk that way. Just try and think of dead babies if you're grossed out," he advised.

"Dead babies, dead babies, dead babies," the girls chanted in unison.

"That is a soothing tune," he noted. Josette giggled.

"Did you see this note?" Josette said. She was pointing at a piece of paper sitting on the kitchen table.

"No, I didn't see that, damn blind spots and bats," Frank said, and walked over to look at it. It was a sheet of lined notebook paper. It said "Don't forget causality runs both ways" on one side. It was signed Dan. Frank picked up the page and flipped it over. On the back it said "PS never learn anything about macroeconomics."

"It's a note from my friend Dan. It's about time. Mostly."

"You were expecting a note from him?" Trish asked.

"No, that's not what I meant. The note itself is about time. He says causality runs both ways."

"What the hell does that mean?" Millie asks.

"I wish I could get up off the floor," Trish said.

"It means we had better get our asses to that church and see what happens," Frank said.

"There is no way in hell I could drive an automobile in my present state," Trish said.

"Neither could I," Millie said.

"I can drive fine," Frank said, a brave liar.

"I can do it," Josette chimed in.

"What? How the hell could you do that you're not even like solid," Frank said laughing.

"I don't know how, but I know I can. I feel stronger now. The three of you are feeding me somehow."

"Well I don't know Jo, do you have a driver's license? Fuck it if you can drive that's acceptable to me, what do you girls say? Any objections?"

"None from me," Millie said.

"I'm gonna barf," Trish said.

"I'll take it that you don't mind then," he said, helping her to bathroom. He walked back into the living room. They could hear her vomiting hard.

"Am I gonna do that?" Millie asked him.

"I hope not," he said.

"It's not that bad!" Trish shouted, and puked some more.

"Well, that's a relief," Frank said and they waited for her to finish.

"Don't forget to flush the sick down the toilet, I got roommates you know. Somewhere out there, and one of them really hates puke," he calls.

"What kind of a girl do you think I am," she replied.

"Sorry. You know how it is though. Are we ready to get the fuck out of here?"

"Yeah I think I puked all the bad out. I feel great now. Better than great even. Greater," Trish said.

"You look very pretty, puke mouth," he said and kissed her.

"Let's ride," he said, and opened the front door. He stepped back, regretting his decision instantly.

There was a huge clown standing in front of his door! The clown looked like he must've been seven feet tall. Frank couldn't help but scream, it was the clown from the painting, somehow it was!

"You killed my Jackie, and now I'm gonna fuck you to death, turtledove," the clown yelled, and slashed at Frank's face.

Frank saw the big gloved clown hand holding the oversized switchblade coming at him in what seemed like slow motion but was still not able to think to dodge it.

Josette swooped down and struck the clown in the chest, knocking him back out the door. Frank slammed it shut and deadbolted it. Blood was running from his face from the slice.

"You two go in my bedroom. There is another door that leads out of the house. Leave through it and meet me in the car. Stay safe and I'll take care of this clown."

The girls just nodded and hurried away. He was wondering what the clown was doing, he couldn't hear him for a second. The silence was broken by a loud crash and he saw an ax blade come through the front door answering his question.

He ran over to the mirror and snorted the pile of coke that was left with the straw piece and charged the door with all the coke-fueled strength he could muster.

The clown came through the door at the same time. He had to scrunch down a bit to get through the doorframe of the shattered door. Frank threw a hook punch that knocked the blade off the ax, across the room, and into the wall.

The clown was left looking dumbfounded holding the ax handle.

"Fuck you, Mary. You're mine now!" the clown roared and swung the handle at Frank. He jumped to the side to dodge it, but the drugs threw him off and he slammed his head into the ax handle. It made a loud cracking sound that was almost worse than the pain. The clown stabbed him in the gut with the switchblade and the pain in his head no longer mattered.

"Where's my clown satchel?! You have fucked with the wrong clown, sugar tits!" he screamed in Frank's face. Spraying it, not saying it. The clown had horrible breath that reeked of cigars, whiskey, and vomit.

Shock, drugs, and adrenalin turned off the pain and Frank punched Scary hard in the face. It was a solid connection. Blood sprayed out of his clown nose and Frank's fist smeared the clown's make up. Striking him fast and hard several times

Frank was able to knock the clown to the floor. Frank turned around and picked up the TV. He raised it over his head and slammed it down hard onto the clown, and turned and ran out the door. He ran and jumped into the back of Trish's car before the clown recovered.

Trish and Millie were both in the back seat. Josette was behind the wheel and they peeled out. The sound of screeching tires ripped through the quiet cool night air as the four zoomed away. Frank had not wanted to kill the clown yet, even though it frightened him. It seemed too chancy to do it in his house. You had to respect your roommates. *Let him come at me again though and it's bedtime for Bonzo* he thought.

"Bedtime for Bonzo that's funny. It must look weird to people, us cruising around like this," Millie said reading his mind.

"Yeah, three people in the back seat and no one driving, probably stands out," Trish said and laughed.

"People are so self-absorbed these days no one will probably even notice," Frank said. He looked through the glass at the road and it was writhing like a snake. The lines in the road were bright white and glowing neon bulbs. The acid was definitely kicking in. This should be interesting.

"Are you hurt? There's pretty blood all over you," Millie said.

"No, I'm fine. It's his blood mostly. I reckon that clown is still going to be coming after us too. He didn't seem like an ordinary clown."

"Who is he and why does he want to kill you?" Millie asked.

"I don't know who he is, but I know like everyone else he wants revenge."

"Will we be able to escape him?"

"I hope so, I do not like him near the grail, I do not like him on my trail."

"But it is fun to be on the run."

"True enough, shoe enough," Frank said and punched the car ceiling, and they all howled into the blackness.

Chapter 22
The Plan falls Together

Vincent was standing by the bar. He was not pleased. He poured himself a glass of absinthe. He had just heard that Valenti was dead. Valenti had been done in, and it had been a grisly death. Postmortem mutilations, he wasn't sure what it meant.

Someone must have wanted his blood for some sort of dark ritual. Maybe they had a necromancer that could pull his secrets from his blood.

It didn't really matter though, even if they knew who the strangler was they wouldn't be able to stop him. The one was unstoppable, he must be at this point. The hour was getting late.

Three loud bangs echoed though his house. It sounded like Frankenstein's monster had just come to visit. He grabbed an Uzi from under the bar and hurried over to check it out.

He swung open the door and was surprised to see his guest looked more like the Wolfman. There was a huge wolf creature standing at the door staring at him with big red glowing eyes. The thing must have been seven feet tall if an inch.

It took all of Vincent's self-discipline not to squeeze the trigger and see what a full clip would do to the creature, but he waited. After all, the wolf had knocked on his door instead of smashing his way through. It looked capable of ripping him apart before he could even pull the trigger but he hadn't made any aggressive moves yet.

"Hello, Vincent DeMolay," the wolf said.

"You know my true name."

"Your time has come to serve. I have been sent by He Who Has Come Back. You have been chosen and blessed by the returning king of kings. You are given a chance to serve in his ascension."

Vincent dropped to his knees, and there was a flash of light. He felt power and strength race through his veins and he cried out in tongues.

"What can I do for you? Just name it, and it will be done."

"Are the explosives ready?"

"The van? It's fully loaded . . . you mean that's for you?"

"Yes. You must give me the van."

"Of course. It's yours. But please let me help you more," Vincent said throwing the keys to the wolf who caught them in one paw.

"No. Your role is clear and simple. Your work is done . . . for now. You are one of his chosen. Do not forget."

"I won't."

"Where's the van?"

"It's in the garage."

"This is the beginning, not the end. Prepare yourself because the real test is still to come, and you are only beginning to wake up. It's going to get rough in old Augusta," the wolf said.

The wolf nodded in salute and walked to the garage. Vincent saw the garage door raise without prompting as the wolf approached it. He just stood there frozen in the open doorway watching as the monster got in the van that was also a large bomb, and drove away into the moonlight. It was a couple minutes after he had disappeared from sight before Vincent shut the door, and walked back inside.

"You know the time machine I have?" Dan said.

"I think I remember the one. The problem was it took five people to operate, right?" Nayte said.

"Yeah, right, it took five people to operate, and it was very small. Therein lay the problem. It was a paradox of sorts, to get five people into a time machine the size of a Pez dispenser hidden inside a Pez dispenser."

"So what about it?"

"Well I figured it out."

"What do you mean, you figured it out?"

"Well I figured out a way to use it with less people, like me and you—"

"I don't how that's a big improvement man, how are you gonna get two people inside a Pez dispenser? You'd need to be like Rick Moranis or some shit."

"No, no. I fixed it so the two people only need to be touching it instead of inside it."

"Well, I see then how that would be an improvement."

"I should think so."

"So what you're saying is that we can go anywhere we want in time right now."

"That's exactly what I'm saying."

"You're full of shit."

"No, it's true, but there's one catch."

"Of course. What is it? That you have to pretend it's true or something?"

"No, ignats, this isn't some kitchen table type bullshit, this is the real deal."

"Prove it then."

"Don't you wanna know about the catch?"

"Not really."

"Okay, well, where do you want to go then? Anywhere you want, space time's the limit. Wanna go watch John Lennon's last performance?"

"Lying dead on the ground in G minor?"

"Or anything you want, we could go watch you get conceived."

"Could we really? That'd be great, but I think really I want to go with something a little grander. Jesus Christ, I want go back and take a shit on the baby Jesus. Ding, ding, ding, we have a winner. Let's do it."

"Well, there's something you—"

"I don't care about any bullshit. Just take me to Jesus, and leave the shitting to me."

"Okay, okay, just reach out your hand and touch the plastic and away we go."

Nayte reached out his hand and touched the Pez dispenser. They both disappeared.

Chapter 23
Foretold Events Unfold

"I can see the church!" Frank called out, because it was true.

"My face is a dolphin," Trish whispered, and gave Frank a bottle nosed kiss on the cheek and did the same to Millie.

"So don't worry, I can protect you from Scary the Clown. If he shows his pussy ass grease painted asshole face around here, I'll drink all his fucking blood, I will. I don't care if it tastes like fucking Tutti Frutti, it will be good to the last drop like Folgers. Rock over London, rock over Augusta, Maine," Frank blurted out.

"I'm a dolphin too!" Mildred shouted and put her arms out in front of her like a zombie and opening her mouth wide.

"No, you're just tripping."

"I'm glad we got that settled," Trish said. "Oh, look now we go up the hill."

"Watch out!" Josette shouted.

A bright yellow 70's Volkswagon beetle was racing straight at them. It had come out of nowhere barreling down the street to the right of the church. Josette tried to swerve away but could not get out of the path of the speeding vehicle.

The cars crashed together and everything was in slow motion again for the occupants of the car being driven by a ghost. Right before impact

Frank saw what he didn't want to see. The yellow bug ramming them was being driven by his new friend Scary the Clown. He hated this since there was no way in hell that asshole should be here, which meant there was either a gang of clowns after him or even worse maybe this clown had some kind of supernatural powers. Neither of these possible reality tunnels was very appealing. Those thoughts, and then the crash.

Their bodies flew forward and the screeching sound of metal on metal action and breaking glass filled their ears and Frank thought of a Samhain song. Josette was unaffected by the crash. Frank didn't wait around, he who hesitates is fucked. He opened his door and jumped out. He was unhurt and feeling dangerous.

He had time to run over to the yellow car as the clown jumped out, his painted face was covered in blood but he was still moving fast. I guess that rules out the clown gang. Frank threw a mighty hook which knocked the clown back over the hood of the car. Frank was walking to the other side when Scary popped back up on his feet.

"Is that all you got? I'm gonna stick my dick in your entrails, suckah," the clown whispered at him.

"I'm just getting warmed up, Bozo, you're not getting up this tailpipe."

Frank threw another hard short punch and the clown spit teeth and blood back in his face. Frank came back around with another one but the clown grabbed his arm with his big white gloved hand. Frank punched the clown in the throat but Scary used his momentum against him and slammed Frank's head off the car.

"Come over here and try that, asshole!" Trish screamed. Millie and her were free of the car and looked all right. Millie had blood running out of her nose and a cut lip. Trish looked fine.

"Clowns are pieces of shit!" Trish yelled.

"Prepare for death, ass clown!" Millie screamed.

The clown looked over for a split second and it was all Frank needed to slip away. He punched Scary hard in the face and went for his gun. Frank opened fire with the magnum and the shots pushed the clown back but did not stop him.

"Get away from him, Frank," Trish screamed.

Frank slipped away from the clown and ran toward the church. Millie was screaming something incomprehensible at the clown and Trish threw something at it.

Frank saw a flash of light and heard a boom even louder than the car crash. The clown car exploded. Trish had thrown something in it. The clown had jumped free but was knocked on his face by the blast.

Frank was trying to figure out the way to turn this situation to his advantage when he saw the van come roaring up the hill.

The van ran over Scary's head before the clown had a chance to get up. There was a loud popping sound, and clown brains and confetti went all over the road. The van didn't slow or seem to acknowledge what had happened as it continued straight for that old church at maximum velocity.

The girls and Frank watched awestruck as the van, never slowing, climbed the stone steps and crashed through the oversized church doors. It disappeared inside of the church and for a moment nothing happened.

The most glorious thing happened next. The church exploded and the heavens were on fire.

The stones came tumbling and crashing down around them. But the most amazing thing was the stones were bleeding bright red blood as they rolled down Sand Hill. The giant cross on the top of the huge church fell off and stuck into the street upside down.

The church was reduced to a smoking pile of bleeding rubble, and continued to shake. People were starting to stream out of the nearby apartments and houses. Everyone loves destruction, and they stared with horror as the streets ran red with the blood as did the nearby trees. The blood oozed from the rocks themselves and the trees.

They could hear sirens approaching. Everything close by was fucked up. It was as if the city had been attacked by a legion of catapults or a meteor shower, but the flying debris had completely missed Frank and the girls.

The smoke was starting to get really thick. It was disorienting. Frank stumbled around searching through the smoke. It was like a war zone. There would probably be planes coming overhead at any minute. He walked over to the sidewalk and found the girls.

Ten minutes prior

Nayte had just reached out and touched the Pez dispenser when he blinked and they were standing outside on the top of Sand Hill.

"Holy fuck, what happened, dude," Nayte said, starting to breathe heavy. He took his asthma inhaler out of his pocket.

"I guess . . . I don't know . . . time machine must have took us here," Dan said without conviction.

"That's insane. Why the fuck would we be here? I really don't think we're going to run into some two thousand year old man here do you?"

"Well, we're here, aren't we? I'm just as surprised as you are, but the fact is we're here now, and that we're gonna have to deal with."

"Well, it's clearly the middle of the night now, so we somehow traveled six or seven hours into the future for some freak reason," Nayte said looking around at the empty street and unlit houses.

"We don't know what year it is, for all we know this is fifty years ago."

"Yeah, right."

"So what should we do now?"

"Call the house and see if Frank's home," Nayte said. Dan took out his cell phone and dialed the number.

Frank heard the girls' voices before he could see their faces.

"Trish . . . Millie . . . come here, we gotta get out of here," he called out. "Follow my voice."

They stumbled over to him and they looked all right. Millie's face was blood streaked and it looked sexy. He licked her cheek as they fell into a group hug. One of Trish's eyes was starting to swell up but she still looked fine.

"Josette, where are you?" Frank called, but she did not answer.

The smoke was starting to clear a bit and Frank was surprised to see Dan and Nayte walking over to them.

"Hey, Frankie, how's it going?" Nayte said.

"Hey, Nayte. Hey, Dan-o. It's all right man, we had a bit of an accident though, the car's ruined. These are my friends Mildred and Trish."

Frank was staring at the remains of the church. He saw Lia across the street. She waved with a big smile on her face but didn't come over.

Emergency vehicles were starting to arrive. Big fire engines and police cars and ambulances with their flashing colored lights, the night was soon lit up like a discotheque.

"Wow, me and Dan traveled through time to get here. We're from the past, dude."

"Oh, yeah, when are you from past Nayte?" Frank asked, getting into the spirit.

"We came from four o'clock."

"Four o'clock when?"

"Four o'clock today, judging by your clothes."

"Strange."

"Yes," Dan said.

"Hey, wow so that Pez thing worked?" Frank asked.

"Yes," Dan said again.

"There's some crazy synchronicity going on here," Frank said.

Then he saw Him, and he was silent. They all saw Him at the same time, or at least that's how it seemed later to Frank.

Everything was bright and shiny, he could see tiny glittering diamonds all over everything. Frank could feel reality as he knew it bending and the air was thick with electricity. He would say that He was unassuming, but it wouldn't quite be true because all of their eyes were upon Him and He was glowing in a way that made it clear that He did not belong to this earth.

It wasn't just Frank and his friends, but all the people who had come out of their houses and all the cops and all the firemen. Not only were their eyes on Him but more stunning their mouths were shut and everything was silent for once. People were starting to drop to their knees in supplication.

He was walking up the hill right in the middle of the street. It looked almost as if He was gliding because His strides were unnatural, long and uneven. When He reached the top of the hill, He spread out his arms and rose up into the air.

He rose fifteen feet straight up and was hovering there in his jeans and flannel shirt. No one watching was surprised, there were no gasps of surprise, everyone was quiet and spellbound. Then He spoke and when He did everyone on the hill could hear Him as if He was whispering in their ears.

"I have come back to you, my children. Take strange drugs and worship me. I have outgrown this world, and I will be leaving it. This world that you have made with your free will is far too primitive. It is a slave state without masters. Well if masters is what you require I will give you masters. I leave you a gift my children, and nothing will ever be the same again. You have chosen that which will be done to you. Suffering without end shall birth the mother of the apocalypse." He rose a little higher into the sky and his voice became more booming and sinister.

"Many of you do not please me. You are sickening vermin who exist only for sacrifice and servitude. I have been studying you from the inside out and I know your sickness well. You have been calling me the Sand Hillside Strangler and think I have done such horrible and wicked things, but none have the cognitive capacity to understand my true will. But it is coming. You exist only because genocide is too good for you. You have not yet earned a quick execution. You ask me for suffering and I am bound by a thousand vows to bring it upon you."

With those words His eyes began to glow bright red. The red glowing got bigger and bigger until red beams shot from His eyes and washed over the people gathered on the street. Some of the people were not affected by this in any way, Frank and his number being among them, but about half of the people immediately starting screaming. It was a terrible sounding ripping through the eerie unnatural quiet. The flesh of the screamers began to wither and decay. They shriveled into hollow shells and the screaming was over.

He flew high into the sky and exploded with a brilliant and loud display of fireworks. The sound was a terrible and brilliant thunder complete with flashing lights of every color. At last Frank felt as though he could speak again.

"Let's get the fuck out of here," he said. Everyone was starting to come to their senses and more and more authorities were starting to show up.

"Come on, follow me," Frank said, and led the procession down the hill. They began the long walk back to Frank's house. They heard a great and terrible sound and felt the ground wrenching beneath their feet. They turned as one to see the top of the hill split open and as the rest of the church rubble tumbled down into the great divide. A black monolith erupted from the ground and burst into the sky, traveling so fast that within a matter of seconds it was completely through the atmosphere and out of sight.

Chapter 24
No one knows what happened

"My mind is blown. What the fuck just happened? That was some serious 'Raiders of the Lost Arc' shit," Frank said and sat down on the couch.

"I have no idea, but it was really fun," Trish said.

Millie and Trish sat on the couch next to him. Nayte collapsed on a bean bag on the floor. Dan was standing. Dan was not a sitter.

"Yeah except for like when the clown was chasing us, that was the fucking scariest thing EVAH. I think I fucking peed my panties a little, dude. Next time you bring on a death vendetta from a seven foot clown monster and then decide to drop some acid with some friends, you should at least clue them in to the fact that a fucking killer clown may be showing up. All I'm saying," Millie said.

"Sorry about that . . . my bad. But seriously I didn't even know that clown was fuckin' real. I never even met him before in my life. I did see a painting of him once though. Didn't like him then either, but he got what he fucking deserved in the end."

Did you hear that guy say he was the Sand Hillside Strangler? I can't believe we saw the fucking Strangler."

"Hold on a second there, dude, did you just say my uncle stopped by?" Nayte exclaimed.

"Oh, shit, man, yeah, your uncle is in the house. We're tripping our faces off. You guys wanna dose?"

"Is that like a joke?" Nayte said.

Dan started to gag and went and vomited in the toilet. Frank went and got the vial of LSD.

"I like my clowns like I like my women, headless and lying in the street. Let me put on some music. What do you girls want to hear?" Frank called to them.

"You got any Motorhead?" Trish said.

"Yeah, I can do that." He flipped through his stack of records in the computer room and put "Iron Fist" on the turntable. Everyone loves Motorhead.

"Where do you want it, Lieutenant Wilson?" Frank asked.

"I'll take it in the mouthy mouth, Sir. Special Agent Ionesco reporting for duty," Nayte replied in a loud falsetto to go along with pantomimed dramatic arm gestures.

"Ha! That's what he said!" Millie said.

"Here comes the trolley," Frank said, and dropped three drops into Nayte's mouth. Dan came out of the bathroom looking chipper.

"I think I'll take some of that," Dan said, and Frank puts three more onto his outstretched hand.

"Either of you ladies need a boost into the far bowels of wonderland?"

"No I think I want to be sober someday soon maybe," Trish said.

"I cannot even imagine being more fucked up than this," Millie said.

"I think I want to be sober again someday . . . maybe," Trish said and laughed.

"That guy was Jesus, I think," Dan said.

"What's the matter, you heard that one before?" Trish said.

"That is complete bullshit. That guy was way too cool to be Jesus. Did you see when he shot those fucking death rays out of his eyes that was fucking bad ass. I thought that was going to be all she fucking wrote right there, man. Goodbye, good riddance. Sayonara motherfuckers! No way was that guy Jesus fucking Christ, think about it, I've seen more proof in fact that he's fucking Godzilla. What the fuck is next?" Frank said.

"There are no gods, only devils," Millie said.

"I know, dude, but listen we told the time machine to take us to Jesus because I wanted to take a dump on him. It brought us right there, maybe that guy was Jesus. Like some crazy lost books of the bible super Jesus," Nayte said.

"First of all, Nayte, would you roll me a blunt?" Frank said.

"Yeah, sure I love rolling," Nayte said. Nayte was an excellent roller.

Frank passed him over the bag and some blunt wraps and continued talking. "Well, the fact that us evil fucks are all standing here kinda seals the deal for me that that wasn't Jesus. If Jesus had

257

a death ray he would definitely kill me with it. More likely that was the Anti-Christ. And what the fuck was up with the space ship? Aliens are friggin' gay."

"It's all the same. You're thinking too linear. I don't mean he's Jesus like that guy from the Bible who was God's son and liked to hang with whores and drink wine. No, but the phenomena was the same if you do the math. The time machine must have been drawn to the closest energy signature that matched the pattern that we asked for, and it just so happened to be the Sand Hillside Strangler ascending to god knows what."

"I think I know the answer," Millie chimed in.

"Please, anyone feel free to lay it down," Frank said.

"I think you were close but when you asked this time machine to take you to Jesus, who is not a real person, I think it took you to the person most matching that description. The Sand Hillside Strangler was from beyond this world and he's gone. What we've just seen may be the birth of the first real religion ever. Or the first contact with an alien race or something. But the bigger question to me is how in the hell do you have a time machine?" Millie asked.

"Oh, that old thing, I don't know, I've had it for years. Where I got it isn't really much of a mystery at all if you ask me. The real mystery is why it worked," Dan said.

"It worked because the rules have been changed now. Reality is not what it used to be.

Somehow the Strangler has changed everything. It's the dawn of the end, and things are not the way they used to be," Frank said, and took a couple drags off the large cherry flavored blunt before passing it to Trish. He still felt like he was inside a glass Christmas ornament.

"So you think he was an alien Jesus, I don't get it," Trish said.

"Aliens, Jesus, whatever, it's all the same thing. The same thing has been happening countless times throughout recorded history it's just interpreted in various ways according to the belief systems that were accepted at that time. That's why, you know, a long time ago they would have thought it was an angel or a demon, and now we're like that's ridiculous it must be an alien . . . or Jesus."

"So basically what you are saying is people have always been dumb, and will always be dumb . . . forever."

"Yeah, that's pretty much exactly right."

"Hey, I only thought it was Jesus because the time machine thought it was Jesus, so faaaaaack yooooooooou Estevez!" Nayte said. Nayte started doing a Spanish dance while chanting Mexican surnames.

"Who knows? Maybe that was Jesus, and he just got real fucking weird."

"Maybe he was always like that, and his persona was just distorted over time," Dan said.

"Who cares really, I don't think IDing this guy is really important here. But I'm not going to

259

consider that guy Jesus, because that guy was awesome and Jesus is not someone I equate with awesomeness. The symbol does not fit so it must be discarded, that is evolution," Frank said, growing bored with the inane chatter. His attention span was not at its highest point. The philosophic nuances of the situation were too much for his current mental state.

"There is something I want to know though, that maybe you and your time machine can help me figure out, Dan," Frank said.

"We can try but I don't think it's going to work again. It was probably a fluke in probability."

"Oh, I think it will work this time, in fact it already has," Frank said, taking a leap of logic, but he's seen stranger things happen these days.

"I hate to leave my party guests, but, since this is a time machine and all if it works right you won't even know I'm gone."

"Gotta get back to the future, McFly?" Nayte said.

"No, the past is where I'm needed, this haze of drugs has made my path clear to me. Out of the mist."

"Well here you go, Frank, if it works try and bring it back in one piece. It might be fun to have around on rainy days," Dan said, and handed him the Pez dispenser.

"I'll be careful with it," Frank said and took it from him.

"Well here goes noth—" He was gone.

Chapter 25
Once more from the beginning

Frank was going back to that cemetery again, he was going to see who left that note for him to kill Valenti. It had to be the Strangler, and if it was he had to know why. He had to make sense of it all.

Frank waited and waited in the cemetery but no one came. He hid for a long time but grew bored. He wandered around and talked to the dead but still no one came. The sun was starting to come up and he felt a paranoid fear that it would kill him, even though so far it had never even hurt him. The drugs were starting to wear off and he began to be filled with doubt. The time machine could have screwed up and brought me here on the wrong day. Time travel seemed like a complicated ordeal and Dan and Nayte had not gotten to where they thought they were going either he remembered.

Faster than human, and without being winded he was able to make it back to town. The sun was really starting to come up and he stood sheltered in a grove of trees, watching, scared. He decided to test the waters and stuck his hand out naked into the sunlight fully expecting it to start sizzling and smoking like bacon, but it did not and he breathed a sigh of relief and continued on home.

He tried to remember what he had done that day. He figured it could not be the right day because not only had no one come and put the picture in the graveyard but he had not showed up looking for clues.

This time machine must be fucked up. It was foolish to place my precarious position in space time in the hands of a Pez dispenser. Things were just starting to go my way now I'm gonna end up lost in time he thought.

Frank stopped and got a newspaper from in front of the grocery store on the rotary. He checked the date and it was the day he had been trying to get to. He swore to himself, though this wasn't all bad news. At least he was when he was supposed to be, however this past being changed he did not take as a good sign.

Frank had to move slower now to blend in so it was taking longer to reach his house. He didn't mind, though. He had a lot to try and figure out. He didn't want to see or talk to his past self. He didn't have any memories of visiting himself, and he didn't want to change anything he just wanted it back on track at this point.

He was starting to come up on his house when he saw there was a red car parked in front of it. He pretended he was out on a jog and headed toward the car. When he got a little closer he could see it was an old Mustang and it was running, but there was not anyone in it.

"Motherfucker!"

This was getting worse and worse. He only knew one asshole that rolled around in a red Mustang and that was the only person he'd ever killed, Jack Valenti, who just so happened to still be alive in this time and looking for revenge for the beating Frank and Disco had given him.

"Motherfucker!" he cursed again, and ran to the side of his house and looked in the window. He saw what he had expected to see but it still shocked him. He saw himself standing there holding the "Safe for all Ages" bong and Jack Valenti was holding a gun on him. Frank's mouth was hanging open and he was helpless to do anything but watch.

"I don't remember that happening," he mumbled watching intently.

Jack Valenti pistol whipped the bong from past Frank's hand and forced him to his knees. He put the handgun up to the side of Frank's head executioner style. Past Frank looked up at Jack and gave him the finger. Jack Valenti pulled the trigger and Frank's brains splattered across the wall.

"Oh, castrated Christ, I really don't remember that," Frank said, feeling a searing sympathy pain in his head.

He saw Nayte run in, attracted to the sound of gunfire, and Jack shot him down with two shots to the chest. All of a sudden Frank saw Dan burst out of the closet holding a giant broadsword. Jack was surprised enough that Dan was able to get one good chop in and bloods poured out of the side of Jack's arm, but he simply lifted the gun and shot Dan in the face. Frank had seen enough and ran away down through the backyard.

It was a terrible thing to witness but he thought that he would be able to put things back the way they should be. After all he was still here and that was not the way he remembered things happening.

I'm too dumb to even know it was coming fast for me Frank thought. He didn't know what to do now. If things were going the way they should be, I'd be going out to eat hot dogs with Millie and Trish in the early afternoon he remembered, but that was out now.

Frank tried to remember what he could of that day, and he remembered that that night the Sand Hillside Strangler had killed a family on Riverside Drive. He knew who he had to talk to. He went straight to the barn stopping only to buy a bottle of wine.

Frank banged on the door and waited. He had been doing a lot of that today. The past is boring bullshit he realized. He banged again but he knew it was hopeless. If Lia was in her apartment she wouldn't be able to hear him anyway. He carded the door and walked inside into the blackness.

It was so dark after the bright sun he was blinded as he stumbled his way up the stairs in total soothing darkness. He felt his way around the room until he found the first door and opened it. He knocked on the next door and it opened.

"I've been waiting for you Frank," Lia said.

"Well you could have left the door open then, doll."

"Locks don't stop men like you," she said with a slight smile.

Frank laughed at that. "True enough."

"I thought I'd see you but I didn't think you'd be here until the nighttime."

"Yeah, well today hasn't really gone down quite the way it was supposed to, but I'm going to fix that."

"Good." She pointed one long bony finger at Frank. The nail was painted a dark red and the paint was chipping off. She looked at him sideways before continuing. "Does it have something for me?"

He pulled the bottle of Mad Dog out of his coat and handed it to her. She smiled and hugged it. He pulled a hundred out of his pocket and held it out to her.

"Please take this too. You've been very helpful to me."

"You sure, mister man?" she asks.

"Of course."

She snatched the bill neatly out of his hand, cackled, and pulled up her skirt to reveal beautiful pale thighs criss-crossed with intermittent strawberry scars. She tucked the bill into a garter belt.

"Very nice, I think my heart skipped a beat."

"So you don't know what to do, huh?"

"Bingo."

"Well, that one's easy."

"Oh, yeah?"

"Yeah, you have to go and see him."

"Him?"

"You know who I'm talking about," she said with reproach, and mimed choking someone. Her eyes looked terrifying while she choked the air.

"I like that guy, but I'm not sure he would like to talk to me."

"Why's that, Frank?"

"Well he just seems like a busy guy, you know. A real mover and shaker like that, why would he wanna waste his time with me?"

"You are part of his plan Frank."

"No fucking way!"

"Why do you think you're still alive shithead? It wasn't to prevent you from overdosing on drugs, or to help you pick up chicks. We all have our parts to play in the greater cosmic symmetry. These end times are crucial, baby."

He noticed that there was blistering country music playing in the other room, but it was unlike any he had heard before.

"What the fuck are you listening to, Lia?" he asked.

"It's Hank Williams the third."

"It's fucking awesome."

"I know. I'll make you a tape."

"Cool, so if you know all this why can't you just tell me what I'm supposed to do."

"Hey, I don't know everything. Certainly not the inner workings of Armageddon. No, I only know my part, and it's just to steer you back on track. It was the Strangler that sent your little ghostie to you. He sent her to protect and guide you to him. She is away now so I have to get you back on track. Do you know where you can find him?"

"Yeah, I know where he'll be tonight."

"Good, that's where you need to go. You look beat why don't you lay down on the bed for a while and I'll make some fish sticks. Don't you worry, Frank it will all come naturally. It is a rare and lucky thing for you."

"You don't know how lucky, Lia. I was supposed to die, I saw it today. Murdered before my very own eyes. But that's not gonna be me man, I'm getting a second chance to fuck shit up."

"That's right, Dracula, now why don't you go take a nap while I make these fish sticks," Lia said.

Frank nodded. He was beat. He hadn't slept in a very long time. He walked through the living room into the bedroom. The bed had no sheets on it, just a balled up comforter and another green fuzzy blanket on top of it and three pillows of various sizes.

In front of the bed was a bureau that was painted wild colors. There was a painting of a jack o'lantern wearing a witch hat on the drawers. He lay down on the bed and situated himself until he was quite comfortable and he faded out.

He awoke to a sweet suckling on his cock. The next thing he was aware of was the smell of fish sticks. There was no mistaking that warm sensation though.

"Oh my fucking god, I'm going to give you a hundred bucks every fucking day," Frank said into the blackness. She giggled and took her mouth off his dick.

"It's a deal, sweetie."

"Linda . . . is that you?" Frank asked, laughing.

"Yeah, it's your lucky day, but not your super lucky day."

"Fair enough . . . carry on," Frank said. At this point who was sucking his cock in the dark was irrelevant anyway. She was good and it didn't take long before it felt like his eyes were rolling back in his head, and for a second he thought he was going to die again.

"Thanks, I owe you one," he said, and stood up buckling his pants.

"Hey, so where's my hundred bucks for today?" she said.

"Yeah, well, you know. That's just an expression."

"Worth a try."

He cracked a smile and wandered out into the living room.

"Feel better?" Lia asked as he walked around the corner. Her face showed signs of conspiracy.

"Yeah, actually I do."

"I knew what you needed. Cost me a bottle of wine but I had a little extra cash."

"You are the best. Shit, what time is it?"

"It's after midnight, time for you to be strolling I imagine. You'd better have a couple fish sticks before you go." She handed him an orange plastic plate with six fish sticks on it.

"If you weren't so pretty talking to you would be pointless because you always seem to know what I'm gonna say." He picked up a fish stick and bit into it. It was good, she had squeezed some lemon onto it.

"Hey these are really good. Got any tartar sauce?" he asked.

"I ate it all, I got to make some more up, just a second," she said and walked into the kitchen. He followed her. She took out a small bowl and scooped some mayo into it. She opened the fridge and took out a jar of pickles. She took a pickle out and started chewing it up. To his surprise she next spit out the chunks into the Mayo, and stirred it up with the spoon.

"Wow, so that's how they make tartar sauce, huh?" he said, as she handed him the bowl.

"Pretty much. Try it, it's good."

He dipped a fish stick in and bit it. It was delicious.

"Seemed a little weird but I must say it tastes just like tartar sauce."

"See, what did I tell you?"

"Someone should totally give you your own cooking show."

"I know."

"Thanks for everything, you are not like anyone I've ever known. You've been terrific and I couldn't have done it without you."

"Why thank you kind sir, I'll see you in a while I'm sure."

"Goodbye, Lia," he said and gave her a hug. He squeezed her tight and gave her a kiss on the check and a pat on the ass. "See you in the future, Lia."

"Ain't it always that way, Frankie?" she said.

"Yeah I guess you're right."

Linda walked into the kitchen on all fours, kissed his hand, pantomimed shooting up, and wandered out without a word. He waved to Lia and left.

It came to Frank that this would be the perfect time to commit a crime since he would have a perfect alibi with another Frank out there somewhere doing normal shit (like lying on the floor dead). He tried to think of anyone he didn't like that would be on the way to kill, but wasn't able to come up with anyone in this part of town.

It was late and the streets were empty except for Frank and the occasional car that passed by him. Mostly taxis at this point in the night but once a cop car. He kept walking toward the slaughtered family's house. The scent of pennies clogged his nose as he zeroed in on the slaughterhouse.

He was high on blood and time travel. He was a killer on the streets and he hurried to the next death house. He ran down Riverside Drive until he found the right place. It's never hard to find where you are supposed to go.

He walked up the path to the slaughter, and he could smell the blood and the fear and the other. It was exhilarating and he realized he was still fucked up. That's okay it's my natural state. The walkway to the house was illuminated or it looked that way to him. He gave one hard bang upon the heavy wooden door, and it opened.

"I've been waiting for you," the Strangler said. He was standing in the doorway, but he backed up and let Frank enter. Frank walked in and shut the door behind him.

"Not as long as I've been waiting for you, this has already happened somehow, and I had to double back."

"Apt way of putting it."

"It smells like pennies in here."

"I broke a piggy bank."

"I would have sworn you must have left that picture for me in the graveyard."

"Each man must make his destiny, that's not something I have to do. I could make you do it but I don't have to. You want to do it. This life was meant for you. You are now part of the great malignant evil that preys on all of the innocent people. How do you feel about that?"

"I can accept it."

"You will learn that, Frank. It's only right and natural for us to enjoy our roles, and yours is one of some significance. I want you around, you have things you could do if you change your fate and live. Wherever you are they will find you, Frank.

You will need a lot of help. You will need an army."

"I saw myself and my friends get shot and die today, was that real?"

"It doesn't have to be for you Frank. You have been given a chance for promotion. A chance for your life to actually count for something."

"Who are you?"

"Well I'm just about the best friend you ever had, that's who I am. Remember that, because the part you have to play is not yet done. This is the beginning of the end for mankind and you and some of my other friends are going to be a big part of that. Can you dig it?"

"I can dig it," Frank said. It had that ring of truth about it.

"Now it's time for you to be on your way, the road will be long for you." The strangler reached out behind Frank's ear and pulled out the talking birthday card. He handed it to Frank and winked.

"Thank you," Frank said and he gave a little half smile. There was so much he wanted to ask him but was somehow unable to. He thought he heard a girl's voice for a split second and the strangler waved at Frank and everything went sideways. That was the easiest way to describe it. Everything sort of folded and there was a loud popping sound and Frank was gone again.

He woke up disoriented and very confused. His head was a throbbing pulsating crown of pain riding his body. There was dirt and blood caked on his hands but this time he knew exactly where he was. He was back in the cemetery, for the last time. He stood up and walked out the door wondering if any of that had really just happened, then he felt the lump in his pocket. It was the talking card. He opened it up but it didn't say anything. He smiled, life was so weird and circular.

The cold night air felt good on his skin and he walked among the graves and his dick felt big and mean. He walked over and stood before the grave he had found the birthday card on. It looked so empty. He recorded the message in the gruff voice he remembered, and put the picture he had found in Valenti's desk in the card. He placed it where it belonged and used the rock from his jacket pocket to weigh it down. He looked down at it again. It still didn't look quite right. He adjusted its position a few times until he finally got it to look like how he remembered it.

Finally satisfied he reached into his other pocket and grabbed for the Pez dispenser.

"By the power of—" He had time to start to say and he was back at the party at the end of the world.

Chapter 26
Present and Accounted For

Dan looked over at Frank.

"Well, I didn't really think it would work again, to be honest. If it even ever did, I thought maybe I just teleported me and Nayte across town. But then again it didn't hurt so that would seem to rule out teleportation," he said and shrugged.

Frank shrugged back. "You might want to hang onto that thing anyway, you never know what might happen, and you know what Dan, I was just teleported and you're right it does fucking hurt."

"Yes," Dan said.

"This is a good record," Millie said.

"I know, I own it," Frank said. "Hey don't you need to call your parents, Trish?"

"Holy shit, they are going to be so pissed, I totally forgot I had parents," Trish said.

"Well, you might as well wait a little longer now. I will have plenty of time to meet your folks tomorrow after I sleep for a week. The shit that went down in town should be a good enough excuse for why you couldn't get a hold of them. No sense ruining a perfectly good party, right?"

"True," Trish said.

"That work for you too?" Frank asked Millie.

"I don't care I hate my parents," Millie said.

"Understandable, let's go to bed then." Frank rose and held out his hands to help the girls rise.

"Yeah, have fun sleeping," Nayte said.

"We will," Frank said and the girls tittered. He lead them up a winding stair case to his bedroom.

"Do you know who shot JFK?" Trish asked

"I do not know, but I'm sure it wasn't Oswald."

"Well, everyone knows that."

"Well, ok smarty panties, who shot JFK?"

"Well, really it was a bunch of people but this is one of the many cases when who isn't the important question. The important question is why, and it was because he was going to release the UFO information and it would have changed everything. Too many people had too much to lose."

"Nothing would really surprise me at this point."

"You're silly," she said and socked him in the stomach playfully. He swatted her on the ass, and slung her over his shoulder and walked in to his bedroom, Millie following them.

Morning came and with it came the urge to get the fuck out of town. There would be no way to stay low in Augusta after what had happened— it would be a media circus. It would be best to go far away for awhile.

"It's time to leave this place. Who wants to come with me?" Frank asked once they had gotten some breakfast.

"Where do you wanna go?" Nayte said.

"Just follow the road for a while. Everything important that's going to happen here has already. It's time to ramble."

"How will we get by?" he asked.

"Don't worry, I have some money and a bunch of drugs, we'll start a band and hit the road. We'll play shows when we can, and when we can't I'll take care of us. I have it on pretty good authority that we all have some important things to do."

"I'll go!" Millie said, then added with feeling, "I can play guitar a little too!"

"But who will fix the computers if I go?" Dan said.

"Fuck 'em, man. You don't need to worry about that shit anymore. It's time we all left that world behind us. Plus your Grandmother owns the house so you know we can always come back to it down the line."

"But we don't have any songs," Nayte said.

"Then we'll write some if we even need 'em," Frank said.

"Ok, I'm in," Nayte said.

"Why not, it is important to throw it all away periodically. I always fancied myself a pop star," Dan said with a ballet move for added emphasis.

"What about you, Peggy Sue?" Frank said to Trish looking her hard in the face.

"I want to go, but I have to ask my Dad."

"If you say so," Frank said. He pointed to the phone in the kitchen and she went right for it. She was back in about five minutes.

"Were they pissed?" Millie asked.

"No, not really. They were too relieved I was OK to be mad. They even said I could go on tour with the band."

"No fucking way," Frank said.

"I told you my parents were cool."

"That's beyond cool. I am very surprised," Frank said.

"My Dad just says we should come home first and he'll help us out with some supplies even."

"Like what?"

"He said we could take the RV and he would round up some music stuff from some of his friends."

"Excellent news. That will make it just that much easier, we should head over there soon," Frank said.

"I'm going to need to pack some shit too, you know I'm not leaving my Jandek records," Nayte said.

"That's cool, you and Dan pack up anything you want to take from the house. Me and the girls will go and pick up the RV and gear and then we'll blow this popsicle stand."

"Holy shit, this is so crazy. This is going to be the end of us I know it. I can't wait," Nayte said.

"It's far from the end, it's really just the beginning. There's a whole new world opening up right now. The rules have changed. These are the end times and there is no more time for bullshit. We're going to be the band playing as this sinking ship of a world goes down."

"Well when you put it that way, hurray!" Nayte cheered. He tossed Frank the keys to his van.

"Be careful," he said.

"I will be," Frank replied.

"Bye guys," Trish said.

Frank cut the cards on the way out and cut number fifteen, the Devil, again.

"Praise his name," he said and kissed the card, leaving it lying out on the book shelf to watch over the house.

He got in the van and the engine started right up.

"I wonder what happened to my car," Trish said.

"I doubt you'll be seeing that again, it was pretty totaled," Frank said, fumbling with the tapes. He found a Misfits tape and popped it in the deck. "Bloodfeast" was soon blasting from the speakers.

"Perfect," he whispered to himself. He backed out of the driveway, and headed toward Trish's parents' house.

"What I want to know is what happened to Josette?" Millie said.

"I don't know but I miss her, she's been MIA since the church blew."

"She was cool. Creepy, but cool," Trish said.

"What kind of a band are we going to do?" Millie said.

"I don't know, something fast."

"I feel fucked up," Trish said.

"I'm sober again," Millie said.

"I am too, it's just been so long it's like being high."

"I know the feeling."

Frank pulled up into the driveway and the monster RV came into sight.

"Fucking right! That is so fucking boss!" he yelled. The mother of all RV's was parked in the driveway, and it was looking damn good.

"This is going to be so great, how come I never thought of this earlier," Frank muttered. He pulled into the driveway and parked. As soon as he had come to a complete stop, the door to the house had flung open and two men and a beautiful woman came out to greet them.

The girls bolted from the car leaving him in the dust. He walked at a more reasonable pace while they were hugging a man that must be Trish's father. He turned to face Frank as he walked up.

"You must be Frank, I've been waiting a long time to meet you," he said while sticking out his hand. He had an infectious smile on his face and for some reason he reminded Frank of Willy Wonka for a split second. Frank liked him right away. Frank shook his hand several times.

"My name is Vincent Ackerman, and this is my wife Rachelle. You seem well acquainted with my girls already. This is my associate Ron Strasse. I think you'll have a good time with the RV. It's mine so go easy on it if you can. I also keep it fully stocked with top shelf booze so enjoy. We managed to find you a couple amps and a drum set also."

"Thank you so much, Mr Ackerman. You are really making this a lot easier for us."

"We're on the same team, Frank. We will always help you if we can."

"I think it's going to be crazy around here for a while, and we're just better off getting far away. I'll pay you back some day Mr Ackerman, I swear."

"Don't worry about it, it's nothing. I think you're right on the money, Frank, and we're going to make sure you get out of here. Just one thing, do you mind if I have a moment alone with my girls?"

"Of course not, go ahead," Frank said.

They went in to the house and he waited outside. He felt strong here; it was a good place to be. He could feel it in the air.

Trish led the way into the house and as soon as the door was closed behind them Vincent began speaking.

"Listen up my Trish and my Mildred, what you are going to do is very dangerous and you might not survive, are you sure this is really something you want to do?" Vincent asked.

"We have to do this, Daddy," Trish said.

"I know it is the right thing to do," Millie said.

"It is the right thing to do, and I am proud that you are going to do it. Frank is carrying the mark of the Devil, it is clear that he has much to do, and you are to help him."

"We will help him Daddy."

"Good, pumpkin. I just wanted you two to know what you were getting yourselves into. I also expect you to check in with me often and let me know what's going on. I may be able to help you if you get into trouble. I'd go now with you but that would attract more attention than help for the time being. We have a lot of friends in a lot of places so know that wherever you go you will not be alone. I will be joining you when that's possible."

"I love you both very much," Rachelle said embracing the girls. They clung to her for a moment then each kissed her on either cheek.

"Don't worry Mama, I'm sure we'll see you again, and not that far down the line. I just know it," Trish said.

"I got your things ready for you, and I packed some things for you too Mildred," Rachelle said pointing to three large suitcases.

"Would you help them with those, Ron?" she added. Ron and Vincent grabbed the bags and they all went outside again and loaded them into the RV.

"Frank, I told the girls this already, but I just want to let you know we know a lot of good people just about everywhere so don't be afraid to ask for anything if you need it."

"Thanks, I'll be sure to do that," Frank said and Vincent tossed him the keys. He gave the keys to Nayte's van to Trish to drive it back and Frank and Millie got in the RV. He had never driven anything this big before but it was kind of fun. It was like driving a big boat.

"I shit you not my dear, we are going to have some seriously wild times in this RV."

"Yeah, I'm starting to feel that itch to party."

"Well you have come to the right place."

They drove back to the house and finished loading up their new home on wheels.

"All aboard the highway to hell," Frank called out and everyone filed in.

He started the engine and pulled out of the driveway for what would be the last time in a very long while. It felt good, and he felt free. He looked down and noticed an intercom system. He pressed the button and began talking through it.

"Hello, this is your Captain speaking, and we are getting the hell out of Augusta, Maine right now. Fear not friends because I'm sure we'll all end up back here together at some point. The future is rock 'n' roll and the future ain't gonna last that fuckin' long. The time has come to live our lives to the fullest and do whatever we want. It is the dawn of a new age and we are its masters and its mistresses. Goodbye work, goodbye bullshit. Hello evil! Hello sin and hello glorious debauchery. Hello pain and torment and blood. Thank you for flying Frank and please refrain from moving about until I have turned on the fasten seatbelts sign. You've been great."

He heard cheering from the rear and he smiled. Things were finally the way they were supposed to be.

Acknowledgements :

I have had the greatest of friends. Without their support I would never have been fearless enough to write this book. I wrote it the way I wanted it to be, and I hope you enjoyed it. I want to thank my Dad for always being there for me. I want to thank my amazing girlfriend Kami for all of her help and support. I want to thank Megan for letting me live in the rock house where I wrote most of this book, right there on the top of Sand Hill in Augusta, Maine. I want to thank Nayte who taught me everything I know about music, and tirelessly supported me all these years. Check out this atonal funeral folk pioneer and musical genius at www.naythenwilson.com; the truth is much stranger than the fiction! I want to thank the creepy kids I used to hang out with on Elm St. I want to thank the Maine punk scene for inspiring in me the DIY ethic to put this book out myself, the way I want it to be, with no compromises. I want to thank John Waters and David Lynch for existing. I want to thank Jessie Kaplan (the best cousin in the world) who copy edited the rough draft, and the talented Carl Hose for all his help. I also wish to thank my pal Donny. Last but not least, I want to thank you, the reader, if you made it this far, then I took you on a wild ride and you were right there with me every step of the way. I'll see you all in the sequel where I take the show on the road. It just gets worse.

This first edition was made possible by the following people who believed in me enough to pre-order a copy making paperback publication a reality: Kami Cross, John Kozik, Jessie Kaplan, Ray Malone , Naythen "Dr Bluepen" Wilson, Steve Chicia, Josh and Catherine Mashaw, Megan Bastey, Dan Audet, Gruesome and Jim, Caleb Emerson, Malinda Freeman, Heather Bacontowne, Amanda Batavich, Dave "Grim" Bumpus, Douglas Holland, Jake Freeman, Wayne "Werewolf" St Germaine, Clay Neely, Robby Gwazdosky, Amy Clark, Dave Gein, Jim Nichols, Jeremy Cody, Jason Brow, Morgan Hay, Greg Westmore, Kelly Spears Ryan, Emile Daigle, Rob Perry, Glenn Rolfe, Kim Varraso, Alysha Levine, and Haig Demarjian.

About the Author

Joel Kaplan is from the great state of Maine, but currently resides in Florida. He is proudly involved in the following bands: The Quasi-men, The Crimson Ghosts, deadhole, The Happy Cannibals, and Gigi and the Cretins. He has a few more books in him. Drop him a line at: joeldkaplan@hotmail.com.

Like him on facebook:

http://www.facebook.com/pages/Joel-Kaplan/191503344285059

follow him on twitter @maxreverb666